TAMING A BEAR

A LION'S PRIDE #11

EVE LANGLAIS

Copyright © 2020/2021 Eve Langlais

Cover Art by Yocla Designs © 2020/2021

Produced in Canada

Published by Eve Langlais

http://www.EveLanglais.com

E-ISBN: 978 1 77 384 180 9
Print ISBN: 978 1 77 384 181 6

CHAPTER ONE

#1 Bear Motto: Never miss a nap.

Warm and snuggly. Soft and comfy. Andrei drooled as he enjoyed a most excellent nap, dreaming of a warm summer day and the buzz of bees.

Until someone poked him.

He ignored it.

A banshee shrieked, but he'd slept through worse growing up. His sister had a particularly annoying pitch. A proper bear could sleep through anything. Even an entire season—which meant, he had to avoid the internet for a while until he caught up on his favorite shows.

Jab.

The pointy end of a finger dug into him. It tickled. He loved a good tickle fight. But that would require waking up and effort. Did he really want to do that when his pillow was so comfortable? Smelled nice, too.

Honey. And woman. And—

The cold water landed on him, a rude deluge that roused him with a roar.

"Who dares ruin my nap!" More statement than query. He shifted from the wet spot and rolled to see the mean person who'd attacked.

"I dare, you hairy beast. Who the hell are you, and what the hell are you doing in my house?" A golden woman glared at him. Hair like honey. Skin smooth and freckled. Expression annoyed.

He smiled. "Well, hello there. I am Andrei Medvedev, and you are?"

"About to whack you with this wrench." Indeed, she brandished a rather large metal tool.

"Is that a wrench, or are you just happy to see me?" He rolled fully onto his back.

"I will beat you with it!" she threatened, holding it aloft.

"Sounds kinky," he drawled, eyeing the woman he'd come to see. She'd not been home to answer his knock, so he decided to wait—inside.

"Who let you into my house?"

"The door."

"It was locked."

"Was it?" he said, all innocence. "You should get a better one."

She scowled. "Apparently. Maybe a bear trap

while I'm at it. "I see it's true what they say about your kind."

"What do they say?"

"Don't trust a bear."

"Nonsense. A bear always keeps his word."

"Says you."

"We are reliable."

"Says the guy who broke into my house."

"You weren't here."

"Then you should have left. Most people call ahead if they're planning to visit."

"But that would have ruined the surprise."

"I'm still waiting for a reason not to brain you with my wrench. Because the more you talk, the greater the temptation."

He smiled at her. Much like other lionesses he'd met, she was fearless. Strong. And cute. "If you murder me, then I can't keep my promise to help you."

"Help me with what? And who made you promise?"

"Would the names Lacey, Lena, and Lenore make it clearer?"

"Those meddling biatches," she growled. "And exactly what did they request?"

"That I assist you in solving a mystery."

"The only mystery is why anyone would think I need your assistance with anything."

"Would you like a list of my skills? I am a fantastic conversationalist. Dancer. Singer, especially after a few gallons of ale. An accomplished pugilist."

"You forgot lock picker."

"I should probably also add gastronomical expert, and master of disguise."

She eyed him. "Given your distinctive size, I find the latter hard to believe. Also, still not seeing what any of this has to do with me."

"Just letting you know ahead of time, given some of the previous minor setbacks."

Her gaze narrowed. "What kind of setbacks?"

"Nothing you need to worry about, Honeybear." He offered a toothy grin.

"My name is Hollie."

"I know." He also knew that she was a bit of a slob who didn't make her bed but had excellent taste in toilet paper. Played Xbox and had a drawer full of tattoo magazines. With her long sleeves, he couldn't tell if she sported any ink.

Maybe she could take off her shirt and show him.

"Hello?" She snapped her fingers. "Would you stop trying to go back to sleep?"

"Not sleeping, fantasizing. About you." He winked. In Russia, panties had been known to hit the floor—or his face—for less.

Her wrench came within an inch of his nose. "In this fantasy, was I beating the hell out of you for being obnoxious?"

"I'll admit, I've never been into violent sex. But for you, I am willing to try."

She growled, and he took that moment—while she contained her passion for him—to stretch. His joints popped, his toes pointing out from under the nest of blankets he'd snuggled into for a nap. The weight of them shifted and bared part of his upper body and calf.

"Are you naked?" she exclaimed, her eyes widening as she stared.

"Very." Now, the panties would come off.

"In my bed!" An excited squeak. Maybe she wasn't wearing any underpants.

"How else would I sleep?" He never understood how there was a market for pajamas. Why waste perfectly good fabric and create more laundry when the naked body slumbered best.

"If you want to sleep in the raw, then do it somewhere else. Now I have to wash everything. Or burn it." She eyed him. "When was the last time you had your shots?"

"I am healthy and strong." He thumped his chest. "Virile, too."

"But obviously slightly addled. Did no one ever teach you it's rude to borrow someone's bed?"

"Not in Russia. And I will point out, I didn't borrow it. It is still here in your bedroom. I merely used the provided amenities while waiting for you. A good thing I got a nap in. You took a long time."

"Because I was working." She glared, waving the wrench. An angry she-cat with claws.

Sexy. He grinned wider, but she didn't appear impressed. "And now you're not."

"You're right, I'm not working. Because I just spent

ten hours on the job. Meaning, I'm tired and not in the mood to deal with a moron."

"Let me handle the moron for you. Just point me in their direction."

She blinked.

He thought of smiling, but given her previous threats about hitting him, he might want to hold off.

"Get up," she snapped.

He lifted the cover and peeked. "Not yet, but if you join me, perhaps we can change that."

Instead of hopping in for a snuggle—or more—she yanked on the sheet, and the cold air hit his warm skin. However, he was proud to say, no shrinkage. Nor any erection. It wouldn't be polite until the lady said, "*yes.*"

"I didn't realize you provided turn-down service. Where's my robe? I prefer cotton over silk, just so you know. It's more absorbent."

"Put your clothes on," she snapped.

"I can't, they're in the wash." He tucked his hands behind his head.

"And why are they in the wash?"

"Because they were dirty." Did Americans need a different reason to wash their clothing?

"Then you should have gone home to change."

"My home is in Russia."

She arched a brow. "Maybe it's time you returned."

"Not until I've restored the honor of my sleuth."

"How is being here supposed to restore anything?"

"It's all part of my promise to help solve the mystery. Did your aunts not inform you yet?"

"We got delayed," said a familiar voice. Lenore poked her head into the room.

"You really told this bear to come here and bother me?" Hollie griped.

"Not in so many words. *Someone*,"—Lenore glared at him—"got here before we could explain things."

"Nothing to explain because whatever shenanigans you're up to, I want no part of them." Hollie shook her head. "So, you can take your bear, your mystery, and your drama somewhere else."

"Don't you get sassy with me. The Pride needs you."

Hollie's lips pressed into a tight line. "The Pride has other people they can call on for special tasks. I don't do that kind of work anymore."

That sounded interesting. Andrei said nothing as he learned more while listening to them talk.

"I know you don't, but these are special circumstances. So, if you're done ogling the impressively sized bear, get your ass downstairs, and we can have a meeting to discuss it."

"Screw your meeting. It's been a long day. I want a shower, followed by dinner, and clean sheets." The last said pointedly in Andrei's direction.

He couldn't resist. "Why this insistence of washing these perfectly fine sheets? Or is this your way of indicating we are going to get dirty?"

The shoe came out of nowhere and clocked him.

"That's my niece, not some cheap floozy," huffed Lenore. Probably jealous. They'd been flirting for years, but out of respect for his good friend Lawrence, he'd never acted on it. To those that might eye askance the age gap, they'd obviously never met the formidable trio of aunts.

"I don't need your help rejecting him, Auntie." Hollie eloquently rolled her eyes.

"I know you don't, but bears are sneaky. Especially this one." Lenore shook her finger at Andrei, and he grinned.

"Who, me?"

"You are every inch your father's son. So get your pants on before I'm tempted to castrate you."

"Can't. My pants are probably still wet in the washer. Unless Honeybear here put them into the dryer." Given her glare in his direction, he didn't think so.

"I am not your fucking maid, and I am not dealing with you. Get rid of him, Auntie, or I will." Spoken with a last wave of her wrench before she whirled and left.

Lenore shook her head. "I don't think she likes you."

"Bah." Impossible. "She's hiding it."

"Deeply, obviously." Lenore snorted. "Find something to wear before she swaps her bludgeon for a knife. Once you're covered, join us in the living room. And for gawd's sake, try and behave yourself this time."

"I've been good," he exclaimed.

"You're naked in her bed."

"She has nice sheets."

Lenore sighed and shook her head. "What was I thinking? This will never work."

He sobered. He couldn't screw up this chance to make things right with the Pride. "I want to help."

"I know you do. Problem being, you know lions and bears don't get along, right?" They didn't, usually. But having met Hollie, he wanted to change that. Her scent tickled him. The woman herself, even more. What an interesting feline. Like a honeycomb found in the woods, he wanted to dig in and see what ooey-gooey sweetness lay inside.

He just needed to be careful that he didn't get stung. That had happened to Uncle Boris. Both his eyes had swelled shut. Blinded, he'd stumbled around and fell off a cliff, landed in a raging river, got swept downstream, and ended up in a water processing planet where he was rescued only a few seconds before going through the debris grinder. His aunt often said that she wished she'd never fished out the sodden lump of fur.

Andrei stood and stretched before yanking the sheet from the bed and wrapping it toga-style around his body, more to protect their delicate sensibilities than anything. Wouldn't want to distract them with his manliness while they dealt with serious matters.

His honeybear was in the kitchen making food, finally being a proper hostess. A good thing. His tummy had a little rumble. He also wanted a drink. He'd ask her after he got fed. Wouldn't want her to burn his meal fetching him a thirst-quencher.

The living room, a comfortable place with a couch he'd almost napped on, held all three aunts: Lacey, Lenore, and Lena. He'd met them years and years ago because of his good friend, Lawrence, a lion who liked drinking and wenching and brawling. Although, Andrei doubted the latter two would happen much anymore given that he'd gone and gotten hitched—to a human of all things.

It just went to show the dreaded M-word, *mated*, could happen to anyone. Anywhere. Anytime.

The very idea. His gaze went to Hollie, who had yet to look his way. Did she not hear him arrive? Did she suffer from an impaired sense of smell?

Lena of the spiked silver hair and handsome features, barked, "Where are your clothes?"

"Washer. Which reminds me. Honeybear," he yelled, "have you put my stuff into the dryer yet?"

The spatula that came flying only narrowly missed his head. He grinned. "She's got great aim."

"She should. I taught her how to throw," Lenore claimed. "Her mother was always shit at sports."

"I never realized you had a niece." Then again, he and Lawrence hadn't talked much about family. He'd only met the aunts because they had a tendency to coddle Lawrence.

"Honorary niece, not blood," his honeybear declared, wandering away from the counter with a splendid sandwich in hand. Judging by his nose, an everything bagel, buttered and layered with processed cheese, mayonnaise, and a poached egg lightly seasoned with salt and pepper.

Almost perfect. He snatched it from her and took a big bite. "Mmm. Next time, though, maybe use some real cheddar, thickly sliced. Ooh, and a few slices of bacon—"

Thump.

Whoosh.

All the air in his lungs left him as she punched him in the gut. Andrei folded, and his snack was stolen!

"My sandwich," he lamented.

"Mine," Honeybear corrected. "If you want one, make it yourself. And while you're in the kitchen, pour me some coffee with a shot of something hard. I get the impression I'm going to need it."

She expected him to not only feed himself but cook for her, too?

He stared.

She took a bite and stared right back.

Sustenance was not forthcoming. "Will you make me something to eat?" He turned his big bear eyes on the aunts. It'd always worked on his mother.

Lacey almost moved, but Lena stopped her. "I don't think so. We're not your maids."

He sighed. Americans. Always so independent. It was why he planned to settle down with a nice, traditional, Russian girl.

Eventually.

And only if his mother approved. He just hoped that

whoever his mother chose could cook and would realize a man sometimes needed twenty-three hours of sleep. Also, she should accept the fact that there was nothing wrong with a grown man sobbing at *Grey's Anatomy*.

With no meal forthcoming, and a rumbling belly, he headed for the kitchen and opened the fridge to see very little inside.

Eggs. Processed cashew cheese. An opened package of bagels. Something labeled *tofu*. "How can you call yourself a cat and not have milk?" How would he eat his cookies?

"I'm lactose intolerant."

Huh. That was unusual in a feline. As he made himself a snack, three bagels, the measly six eggs left, a tankard of coffee for himself—and a dainty tea for his honeybear because caffeine would put hair on her chest—he headed back to the living room and the arguing.

"What do you mean you volunteered me? I don't do security anymore," Hollie declared.

"But we need you," Lacey stated, spreading her hands.

"The Pride has plenty of people who can go on a wild goose chase."

"Not really. Arik,"—the Lion's Pride king—"has them dealing with some kind of emergency. Those who are left..." Lenore's gaze slewed to Andrei. "Let's just say it didn't work out."

"Because of the bear." More stated and less question. Hollie shook her head. "Even if I were to agree to help, I wouldn't want his assistance. I work alone."

Rather than reply, Andrei ate.

"I know you usually do, but he volunteered," Lacey stated.

Lena snorted. "More like he begged for a way to avoid war, given what his stupid sister did."

The reminder almost made him lose his appetite. Lada, his spoiled brat of a sister, had betrayed his sleuth. She'd actually attacked one of the Pride. Idiot. And then, she'd compounded her crime and guilt by fleeing. He had to do something to restore their honor. What better way than to volunteer his incredible mind and body to help the lions solve a mystery involving a very old key.

"How is that Neanderthal supposed to help me?" Hollie remained unconvinced and basically called him dumb. He'd take offense, but his snack might get cold.

It was Lenore who argued on his behalf. "Given the key originated in Russia, he might be able to get you into places that Peter couldn't." Peter being the human who'd located the strange key that unlocked... what? That was the question. Especially since his sister and others had been willing to resort to violence to get their hands on it.

That got Lena to snort. "Peter is an idiot, who is probably lying."

Lenore nodded. "I agree. The man knows more than he's saying, but Lawrence expressly forbade us from laying a claw on him." Probably because Lawrence was married to Peter's sister.

Andrei paused in his inhalation of food to comment. "I didn't promise. Want me to make him talk?"

"Thanks for the offer. But, no." Lacey patted his arm. "Asking you to do it is the same as breaking our word."

"Besides," Lena interjected, "if that moron could figure it out, so can our super-smart niece."

"Flattery won't win this argument. I don't want to do this. Don't have time, either. You do realize, I have a job. I can't just go haring off, looking into some stupid key."

Lena smirked. "I knew you'd say that. Which is why I handled all your appointments for the next week."

"You did what?" Honeybear exploded. "How dare you screw with my clients?"

"You misunderstand. *We* are your clients for the next week. Or did you not notice the names?" Lena remarked.

The statement had Hollie rising from her chair to head for the front hall, where she grabbed a notebook and flipped. Frowned. Turned some more, then glared.

"You guys booked up my entire week on purpose?" She tossed down her agenda, and Andrei glanced at the open page. Monday at nine, G. Ivgotapee, full toilet replacement. Tuesday, snake the lines at H. Otshouer.

He snickered.

Honeybear cuffed him. "This is not funny."

"You have to admit, those are clever."

"Thank you," Lenore said. "I was most proud of Thursday's appointment."

A peek showed it as Dr. Ayndatub. And that was when he finally clued in. "You're a plumber."

"And?"

He blurted without thinking first. "You're a girl."

That got him a cold stare. Frigid enough that he wanted to get back under her soft covers.

"Just because I pee sitting down, doesn't make me incapable of doing my job."

"You pee sitting down?" Lena interjected. "Did your mother not teach you how to go while standing and keeping your feet dry?"

Hollie slewed a glance at her aunt. "Not all of us feel a need to use the men's washroom in public."

"The women's ones always have lines," Lena grumbled.

Beep.

The strident sounds had him eying the door that hid the washer and dryer. Could it be? Had his honeybear chosen to surprise him?

"Did one of you put his clothes into the dryer?" Hollie asked.

Only Lacey appeared sheepish. "He needs something to wear other than that sheet."

"Don't be so hasty," Lenore murmured with a wink.

Hollie gagged. "You are old enough to be his mother."

"Young mother. And, so what? Age is a state of mind," Lenore declared.

"My father never let a difference in years get in his way." Andrei decided to help since Lenore appeared to be on his side.

"Your father's lust is why he's in jail," muttered Lena.

"Your father is a pedo?" Hollie's nose wrinkled.

He quickly explained. "Bigamist."

At her glance, he shrugged. "He loves getting married. Unfortunately, he has a tendency to forget that he needs to get divorced first."

"And this is who you want me to work with?" Hollie huffed, grabbing the tea he'd made for her, grimacing and then slamming it down before stealing his tankard of coffee.

He might have protested, but he didn't mind the thought of her lips touching the same rim as his.

Lacey had opened the bifold door to the laundry room and pulled out his clothes, tossing them in his direction. He caught them and put the warm fabric to his face.

"You're supposed to wear them, not sniff them," Hollie declared.

"With pleasure." He slid on the still-hot clothes with a sigh. When he was done, he noticed Hollie and her aunts had turned away, except for Lenore, who peeked and winked.

"I have covered my magnificence, you may feel free to look without being overcome with lust," he declared.

"You wish," Honeybear muttered. Only to exclaim, "What happened to your clothes?"

"I am being fashionable," he said of the many tears in the jeans and t-shirt. No point in mentioning that he'd had some trouble leaving Russia.

He just hoped it didn't follow.

CHAPTER TWO

Even though he'd covered most of those slabs of muscle with clothes, Hollie still found herself distracted. It didn't help that she kept picturing him in her bed.

The first man to ever grace it.

Not that she was a virgin. She just hadn't had a serious boyfriend since college. No interest. No time.

Still, if even a Neanderthal could attract, then obviously she needed to get laid—by someone who wasn't an annoying Russian bear.

An ursine she was stuck with because her aunts had concocted some plan that involved some mysterious key.

Speaking of which... "Where is this key you all keep yapping about?"

"Does this mean you agree?" Lacey asked, only to have Lena punch her in the arm. "What?" exclaimed Lacey. "I was just asking."

"Don't push me," Hollie growled. She already felt stressed enough as it was. Her plans for a quiet evening, eating a sandwich, maybe playing Animal Crossing were dashed. At the same time, she couldn't deny her curiosity.

"We don't know much about it other than it's old and doesn't appear in any online database." Lena snapped her fingers, and Lacey reached into the pocket of her pale pink cardigan. Where Lacey was all prim and proper, Lena was the tough-looking aunt, and Lenore the voluptuous, slutty one without any sense of style. And not real aunts, but self-proclaimed ones, given their close ties to Hollie's mother.

Lacey held up the key, and Hollie was under-whelmed. Old, dark metal with some carvings. It didn't ooze magic or evil.

"How do you know it's important?" She held out her hand to touch it, only to see a giant paw snatch it.

"Hand it over, you giant oaf." She showed her palm in demand.

"In a moment, Honeybear. Do you know this is the first time I've actually gotten to see it up close?"

"Because we couldn't be sure we could trust you after what your sister did," Lena scolded.

"What did his sister do?" Hollie asked.

"She wanted this key so badly, she took our sweet boy Lawrence and his mate prisoner!"

"Oh." Hollie could now see why the ursine might want to put things right.

"I am not my sister. I am a bear of honor," Andrei declared.

"We'll see about that," was Lena's ominous reply.

"What can you tell us about the key?" Lacey asked.

Hollie waited for him to say something dumb, like maybe it opened a lock.

But the bear took on a pensive cast. He rolled it between his fingers. "It is old," he declared. He squinted at it. "The images are vaguely familiar."

"Russian in origin?" Lenore queried.

"Parts of it, maybe." He brought it to his mouth for a lick that made Hollie grimace, then put it between his teeth for a chomp.

"Don't wreck it," Lena shouted.

"It's mostly iron," he stated. He licked it again. "Not conductive. About three centuries old, I'd say, given the blend of metals. While the workmanship is reminiscent of European key makers for that time, the design is not."

Hollie blinked at him. "And you know this how?"

"I grew up with old things."

"You shouldn't talk about your mother that way," Lenore remarked with a smirk.

He arched a brow. Thick and full, like his head of hair. "I would never disrespect my mother. She is the toughest person I know."

"Says the man who thinks it's okay to take naked naps in strangers' beds," Hollie muttered.

"I wouldn't have expected a niece of yours to be

such a prude," he said in her aunts' direction and shook his head.

"Not all of us feel a need to flaunt," Hollie argued.

"If you are uncomfortable, don't look."

How could she not? The man was built like a brick house of muscle.

"Children, if you're done bickering," Aunt Lenore interrupted, "let's get back to the key. Surely, your sister said something to you about it, given her intense interest."

Andrei shook his head. "Nothing. I never even knew Lada was involved in Lawrence's kidnapping until after the rescue operation." A good thing his sister had gone into hiding, or he'd have murdered her himself. What had possessed her to betray everyone like that?

"And still no word on her whereabouts?"

"No. And we've been looking."

"Have you?" was Hollie's doubtful reply. "Would you really turn in your sister?"

His dark gaze turned momentarily somber. "She needs to answer for her crimes against the sleuth. She endangered us all. That can't go unpunished."

Could be he told the truth. Or was this a case of him looking for a chance at the key? To succeed where his sister had failed?

She voiced her suspicion aloud. "How do we know we can trust you? Maybe your offer to help is a ploy to steal the key the first chance you get. Or perhaps you want to use us to solve the mystery."

"I can only give you my word that my intentions are honorable."

"Your word," Hollie scoffed.

"It's all I have," was his somber reply.

"I've known Andrei for a long time, and I will vouch for him. While he can be dumber than a rock, he is also loyal and steady." Lenore complimented and elegantly insulted in one fell swoop.

"Good for him. I'm sure he'll make someone a wonderful partner then. Someone else. Because I can't help you. I'm a plumber, not a detective," Hollie reminded.

"Now, you are. But you used to be the best hunter in the Pride."

Used to be because she'd gotten tired of the drama. She wanted a steady life. The kind where she got to sleep in her bed at night and not in a wet ditch or on a windy rooftop. Taking care of the Pride was a full-time job that could demand her attention at any hour of any day. As a plumber, *she* decided her hours.

"I get that the Baddest Biatches are busy. But in that case, why aren't you taking care of it?"

The aunts tossed each other a quick glance before providing three bullshit excuses as to why they couldn't and why it should be Hollie.

"My passport expired," was Lacey's bullshit excuse.

"I've got jury duty," was Lenore's.

"Can't," came Lena's simple reply.

Hollie rubbed the spot between her eyes. "Listen, I get that you want help, but—"

"Please."

The word, uttered softly by her gruffest aunt, was the biggest arm tweak of all.

"Fine."

"Most excellent." Andrei rubbed his hands together, drawing her glare. "I sense we shall make excellent partners."

"I said *I'd* help them with the key. I don't need your assistance."

"Think of him less as the help and more like...security," Lenore stated. "People are desperate for this thing. Once they find out you've got it, you'll be in danger. He can protect you."

"I can protect myself."

"Hollie." Just her name said in a warning tone, but it was a reminder that there was such a thing as being too stubborn.

She sighed. "If he pisses me off, I won't be held responsible."

"Just keep him fed, and he'll behave," was the advice from Lacey.

"Now, to give you a head start with the key, we're going to pretend that we still have it in our possession," Lena informed her.

"You really think someone will come after me?"

"Yes." The three seemed in agreement on that.

"Any ideas where I should start looking for answers?"

"No."

Hours later, after getting the whole story—which didn't amount to much—she realized that they really weren't going to be any help. The key and the pursuit of it comprised most of the info, and that did nothing to help pinpoint its origin.

Hollie yawned. "I think I'm done for the night. I'll start looking into it tomorrow." As she saw the aunts to the door, Lena leaned close to whisper, "I know you're not happy about having him around, but he's the only connection we have to Lada." Left unsaid was that the Pride really wanted to get their claws on her, which also probably explained Andrei's insistence on being close to the investigation.

The door shut, and Hollie turned to look up, and up again, at the giant man towering behind her.

"Do you need a lesson on personal boundaries?" she asked.

"Do I make you uncomfortable? Would you feel better if you fetched your wrench?"

"You don't scare me." He didn't. However, he did discomfit. He made her feel things she shouldn't. Which annoyed her.

"I'm glad to hear that because I would never harm you."

"Let me guess, because I'm a woman."

"Partially. But mostly because you are not my enemy. And even if you were, you're not even half my size. It wouldn't be fair."

"Meaning if we get into a fight, you'll only hit

people the same size as you?" She eyed him. "Doubt that happens often."

He grinned. Mischievous and much too cute. "Fear not, Honeybear, you won't come to harm while I'm around."

"No, I'll just have my food stolen."

"Sharing is caring."

"And a fork can be used as a weapon. Remember that the next time you eyeball anything I want to put into my mouth."

His gaze went to her lips. "Understood."

She almost squirmed, even as his reply had nothing inherently sexual about it. "Good. Now, if you don't mind. It's late, and I'm tired. I trust you can see yourself out." She headed back to her living room to drop onto the sofa.

"I can't leave."

"I promise you won't miss anything, as I won't be working on the mystery key until tomorrow. So be here at nine a.m. for our visit to the history department at the university."

"Wake me at eight."

"Ask room service to do it."

"You have room service?" His expression brightened, and she got a sneaky suspicion.

"What hotel are you staying at?"

"Here."

"I am not a hotel."

"Can't guard you if I'm not close by. Weren't you paying attention to the part where your aunts said that this key is dangerous?"

"I don't need protection since no one knows I have it."

"They will once you begin your inquiries."

She sighed, already exhausted by the drama. "I am not in the mood to argue. You want to guard me, then fine. But you'll regret it. I don't have a guest bedroom."

"Sharing is fine with me."

"We are not sharing my bed," she growled. "You want to sleep here, then you get the couch. With clothes on!"

"I can't sleep with my pants on."

"Try. Goodnight." She stalked off to her bedroom, mostly to escape him before she was tempted to help him get undressed for bed.

She brought the key with her. With her nerves wound up—and her blood pumping with irritation—she started with some basic online searches.

Old keys. Missing keys.

Way too generic to get anything.

She took pictures of the key next and ran more searches, using a few sites that could take an image and compare it to billions of indexed files.

Nada.

She eyed her bedroom door and wondered if her guest was sleeping yet.

With clothes or without?

She could use a snack. Her hand was on the knob before she realized that she'd found herself an excuse to look. She tucked it behind her back. She couldn't go out there. He might see it as an invitation. Instead, she drank a glass of water and prepared for bed, going to sleep with the key in hand.

She spent the night tossing and turning. Plagued by strange nightmares.

The kind she'd not had in a while.

Struggling and chattering against the cold until a warm blanket wrapped around her, and a voice soothed, *"Shhh. I have you..."*

She slept soundly until dawn brightened her room. She blinked and stirred, wondering what had happened to her bed. Then it rumbled, "Morning, Honeybear."

CHAPTER THREE

Usually, Andrei needed help getting ladies out of his bed, but Hollie couldn't jump out fast enough.

"What the hell?" she squeaked. "What are you doing in my bed?"

Nothing since he was a gentleman. "Has anyone ever told you that you're a lousy sleeper? Talking and thrashing, disturbing a bear's rest."

"Do not," she huffed.

"Oh, you definitely do. But turns out the solution to us both getting some sleep was simple. You just needed a snuggle."

She frowned. "You can't just invade my room like that."

"Hardly an invasion. I told you I'd protect you. Apparently, that includes bad dreams. Want to talk about it?" Because he'd only gotten a sense of fear from her. No coherent words. He didn't need any. From the moment he'd heard her first low moan, he couldn't help but go to her. Comfort her. Worried when she didn't wake at his touch. He'd drawn her into his lap, wondering if he should call for help, when she calmed. Nestled against him as if she belonged.

"I don't remember it." She turned from him, tense and beautiful in her t-shirt and shorts. He caught a hint of ink peeking from her thigh. And on her forearm, more color. Not an easy thing to accomplish, given that shifter bodies rejected and regenerated in ways that made tattooing challenging—and painful.

"Are you afraid of something?" he asked. "Do I need to hit someone for you?"

"I am not in the mood to be psychoanalyzed. Nor do I appreciate you coming into my room while I'm asleep to maul me."

"Hardly mauling. I comforted, and you clung to me like a lemming. Wouldn't let me leave. Do you hear me complaining that I had to bear your weight all night or that you drooled on my chest?" He pointed to the bare skin. Drew her gaze.

Her cheeks flushed. "You better not be naked under those blankets again!"

"In deference to your delicate sensibilities, I kept my boxers on. See?" He flung back the sheet to prove it.

She glanced, and her gaze strayed long enough to notice the tenting.

"You're disgusting."

"You'd condemn a man for having to take a piss?" Only partially true. After all, a weak bear could only restrain himself so much, especially around this woman. Everything about her fascinated him, from the way she stood up to him, to how she huffed hotly when she slept.

Did she understand the kind of restraint it took to keep his paws to himself, especially when she squirmed atop him?

"If you need to pee, go now. Because I need to shower, or I'll be late for my appointment."

"*Our* appointment," he corrected. "Who are we going to see?" Andrei rolled out of bed, unable to prevent a stretch of his limbs that once more drew her gaze—and heated her cheeks. She moved to her dresser and began slamming drawers as she grabbed clothes.

"Going to see a friend of mine, who might be able to give some insight on the key."

As Andrei entered the bathroom, he caught himself before asking if that friend was male or female. He didn't close the door as he relieved himself, and his prudish honeybear yelled, "What is wrong with you? Did your mother never teach you any manners?"

He washed his hands before emerging to say, "She taught me that bodily functions are natural and nothing to be ashamed of."

She glared at him. "Close the door because I have no interest in listening to it."

"Don't tell me you're the type who won't fart in front of a man because she thinks he'll be disgusted."

"I don't fart because it's gross."

"Everyone farts," he stated.

"Not me. Now, if you'll excuse me, I need to shower." She swept past him, head held high, arms full of clothes.

He couldn't help but needle her. "Want me to join and wash your back?"

She stumbled at the threshold as she muttered through gritted teeth, "No."

It proved an interesting torture to think of her in the shower. Naked. So, he distracted himself, wandering around her place, enjoying the scent of her and the glimpses of her personality he found.

Her video games ran the gamut from role-playing types with magic and monsters to one that seemed to be about farming. No books, other than a few tomes on a desk about how to run one's own business. The computer was password protected.

The art on her walls was generic stuff: scenery of cities and landscapes. No pictures of her or anyone else.

When she emerged, wearing a towel on her head and fully dressed in pants and a long-sleeve sweater, he had a turn in the steamy bathroom, the scent of her making him close his eyes and handle the stubborn erection that had returned.

When he emerged, feeling refreshed—and more in

control of his body—he rubbed his hands together and exclaimed, "What's for breakfast?"

She sat on the couch with a cup of coffee and her phone. "Nothing, because you ate everything last night."

"Then let us go dine somewhere. My treat." While his clothes hadn't survived his trip all that well, his credit card had.

"Isn't that the same outfit you arrived in?"

"It's still clean."

"Your pants and shirt might be, but you slept in that underwear." Her nose wrinkled.

"Don't worry, Honeybear. I tossed those into the laundry basket."

The moment she clued in, her gaze dropped, then rose quickly. "Do you seriously not have any other clothes?"

"My luggage didn't make the trip." He'd been lucky to get on the plane himself.

"You'll need to go shopping, then."

"Where?"

"In a store." She rolled her eyes.

"We will go after our meeting."

"What's this *we* thing? You don't need me to do that."

"Firstly, I am a visitor to your city. Meaning, you are more knowledgeable about where to go. Second, I cannot leave you alone, so either you come with me, or I will continue wearing the same clothes every day, further meaning they will require frequent washing. And given nothing you own will fit me..."

He could see the gears turning in her head as her face flushed. "We will hit the mall on the way back from the university."

They ate first at the diner up the street. She chose a small breakfast of three pancakes, two sausages, ham, scrambled eggs, potatoes, toast, orange juice, and a coffee. He had four of the steak breakfasts, two omelets, plus a Belgian waffle with whipped cream and fruit.

As he finished it off and debated getting a pastry, she eyed him. "Do you always eat like that?"

"Like what?"

She cradled her coffee. "Like there is an alien universe living inside you, feeding off whatever you put down your gullet?"

"I'm a growing boy."

"You're a man in his thirties."

"Exactly. Just entering my prime."

She shook her head but smiled. "I would need three jobs to pay for groceries if I ate like that."

"In Russia, our compound has a large garden and hunting to supplement. We also run a food supply and distribution service and get much of our goods at cost."

"Wait, did you just say you deal in groceries?" She blinked.

"Yes."

"But..." She eyed him, then frowned. "You're a Medvedev. I thought you were crooks."

"Not so much thieves as black-market dealers."

Her lips pursed. "Dealing in what? Drugs?"

He laughed. "Not even close, Honeybear." He leaned forward. "We deal only in things you can eat. People pay a lot for rare delicacies. Which is why I must mend the rift caused by my sister's actions. The Pride is our biggest client. Or did you think the high-quality catnip your chefs like to use can be bought off a store shelf?"

"So, you *do* deal in drugs!" she accused.

"And occasionally, toilet paper. If there's a demand, we supply it."

Breakfast eaten, paid for—including a large tip—they then took Hollie's plumbing van to their next destination. As she drove, he eyed the back with interest. Neat and tidy, with her tools carefully arranged and displayed for maximum efficiency. The name on the truck was simple: Holly Jolly Plumbing, with a smiling plunger. A woman with a career, and not in a traditional area.

"Why become a plumber when you could have had a job with the Pride?" Their business interests spanned the world.

"I had one with the security division for a while. But I wanted something a little less hectic."

"Then why not transfer to one of their other divisions?" Because the Pride had their furry paws in a few businesses.

"Hair products and foodservice don't interest me."

"But plumbing?" he asked, still confused by that choice.

"Why not?"

"Because it's a dirty job that most people wouldn't necessarily think of learning." The blunt truth.

"Exactly." She turned into the visitor parking lot for the university. "A lot of high school kids make the mistake of going for interesting-sounding degrees. I did my research and figured out what there was an actual demand for where I could be my own boss."

"So, you'll work with shit, but don't believe in farting?"

She glanced at him as she put the truck in park and turned off the engine. "I put up a Christmas tree, but that doesn't mean I expect a fat dude dressed in red velvet to put anything under it." She exited before he could reply.

A good thing since he couldn't actually think of a snappy comeback. Mostly because he'd meant to put her off-kilter, and she'd turned the tables. Most excellent.

He followed as she took off with a quick stride, and enjoyed the tight wiggle of her ass in the jeans she wore, hugging her lithe frame. She lacked the usual curves he generally went for, and yet, her femininity was clearly displayed.

The university campus looked like many others, sprawling over a few acres. The buildings were dated brick in some places, and more modern stone and siding where new additions had been built. They headed for an older, smaller building.

"Did you get your plumbing degree here?" he asked since she seemed familiar with the place.

"To the appalment of many, I went to a trade school. Paid my own way, too."

"Doesn't your Pride provide scholarships?" The sleuth did to those with the ambition and grades. Which wasn't many. Bears preferred napping to studying.

"Mama taught me to never take what I didn't need. So, I saved during high school and worked weekends and evenings for the time I attended. Then I apprenticed the first few years before branching out on my own."

"Impressive." It truly was. Few in his sleuth preferred working to a free ride.

Andrei was somewhere in the middle. Work hard and sleep hard in equal measure.

"So, who is this person we are going to see?"

"Professor Kline. He specializes in European history."

"Is he...?" He left it unsaid, but she understood.

"He's one of us, which means we can be open."

"Can he be trusted?" Because Andrei only had to recall his sister's actions to realize that something about the key brought out the greed in people.

"Ted won't tell anyone."

Ted? She knew this professor by his first name.

The reason why became apparent when they walked into his office.

Professor Kline wasn't a stodgy old bastard in a cardigan. He was a young and handsome man, with a wide smile, a feline scent, and a face Andrei wanted to punch—especially once he realized that Hollie and this Ted used to date.

CHAPTER FOUR

For some reason, Andrei glowered at Ted. Hollie couldn't have said why. He'd done nothing but say hello and give her a quick hug as they exchanged polite pleasantries.

Hi, it's been a while. You look great. Blah. Blah.

Sulking, Andrei quietly hulked in the background, quiet for once, meaning she could get to business.

"I need your help with something. I've recently come into possession of a key," Hollie announced, pulling out her phone. She brought up the images she'd taken of the artifact. And the video.

Ted glanced through them before saying, "Can I see it?"

"Nope."

You didn't bring it?"

She shook her head. "Sorry. The aunties wouldn't let me borrow it."

"Do you think they could make an exception? It would really help to see it in person." Ted frowned.

"I can ask them."

"Please do, because while images are well and good, there are small details that might only be perceived in person." Before he could say anything else, there was a knock at his door.

"Excuse me a minute while I handle whoever that is."

Ted wasn't gone long. When he returned, he headed for a bookshelf, where he pulled out a few tomes. He began leafing through pages, and she couldn't help but ask, "Do you recognize it?"

"No. However, the style is reminiscent of the sixteenth century." He stopped on an image and turned the book to show her. It was vaguely familiar in the sense that the key on the page was big, metal, and ornate.

"Any way of pinpointing who made it? Or what it opens?" she asked.

Ted laughed. "Do you have any idea how many hundreds of keys were created in that time? It could be for anything. A treasure box, a door, a keepsake. I'd need to have it for a few days to run some tests."

She shook her head. "That won't happen. There have been...issues surrounding it."

"Issues, like?"

"Let's just say some people really want to get their hands on it and aren't afraid to use violence to do so."

That brought a frown to Ted's face. "Are you in danger?"

"She's fine," grumbled Andrei, finally taking an interest.

"And you are?"

Before she could reply that he was the ball and chain given by her aunts, he said, "Boyfriend."

She blinked and opened her mouth to refute the statement, only to see him staring at Ted. No, not staring. Glaring.

What the hell? He appeared jealous. But how did he even know? Why would he care?

"Congratulations. Hollie is quite the catch. Unfortunately, I was too dumb to realize it in college." That was a lie. Ted had issues with monogamy. Hollie had broken it off and likely would have never spoken to him again. Unfortunately, he belonged to the Pride, and being mad would have indicated that she cared.

She didn't. He'd just provided a warm body to use when she needed.

"I have to agree, my honeybear is special," Andrei declared.

"If we're done discussing me, can we get back to the key?"

Ted shook his head. "I'm afraid there's not much else I can do for you. I mean, unless you know what family it originally belonged to."

"How would that help?"

"In the case of important heirlooms, there's usually a family legend passed down about it. As it is, I couldn't tell you if it's for a door, a piece of furniture, or even a chest."

"Meaning it's like a needle in a haystack." She sighed.

Ted shrugged. "Sorry I couldn't help you more."

"It's fine. Thanks for your time."

They left, no more ahead than when they'd started. Frustration meant that she felt a need to snap, and Andrei provided the perfect target.

For her fist.

"What the hell were you thinking, telling Ted you're my boyfriend?"

He didn't gasp or cry, just rolled his massive shoulders. "I was simply giving you a cover. It looks less suspicious if your boyfriend is sleeping over than a bodyguard."

"How would I have a boyfriend from Russia since I've only rarely left this state?"

"Online dating."

"No one would ever believe I'd use it."

"Mail-order Russian groom?" He grinned.

"As if I'd have chosen the largest one in the catalogue. Not to mention, do I look desperate to you?"

"You must have been at one point, given you dated that pinhead."

"There's nothing wrong with Ted."

"He's slick."

"But good in bed." She felt a need to toss that in, and the reaction was a bit more than expected. They'd reached her van, and she suddenly found her back against it, his hands and arms framing her as he leaned down, his face level with hers.

"What are you doing? Get out of my space." She pushed on his chest. To no effect. He moved closer and whispered, "We're being watched."

"What? By who?"

"I don't know, but they've been tailing us since we left the history building."

"Could be a student."

"Maybe. But just in case, kiss me."

"Why?"

Rather than explain, his mouth touched hers, and her senses exploded.

Her lips clung to his. Her breaths shortened, and heat curled and tickled between her thighs.

When the kiss suddenly ended, it took her a moment to open her eyes. A second more to see Andrei looking over his shoulder.

"Good job playing the part," he said. "They're gone."

Playing?

There was nothing fake about her wet panties and the strong urge she felt to grab him by the ears and yank him back for more.

The very idea meant she snapped a terse, "Let's go."

"Where to, Honeybear?"

If she said her bed, he'd probably agree.

So instead, she did the one thing sure to cool her ardor. "Time to hit a mall for some clothes."

Frazzled by the kiss, she didn't say much as she drove. She only half-listened to the bear at her side until he said something interesting.

"Rewind. What was that last bit?"

"Your professor said something about family legends."

"Do you know of one with a key like ours?"

"Not exactly. However, there is a symbol on it. It feels...familiar somehow. Like I've seen it before."

"Which one? Where?" Could the caveman by her side actually prove useful in this hunt?

"I will ponder it over lunch." The all-you-can-eat buffet owners might have had to declare bankruptcy if Andrei hadn't insisted on paying extra. For all he was big and brash, and an unabashed dealer in forbidden food, he had a strange code of ethics. It meant that he didn't skimp on paying for service. Held open doors for her. Remained standing until she sat.

And kissed her so well, she kept staring at his mouth. It currently moved, but it took her a second to realize that he was addressing her.

"I said, do you mind if I send a picture of the familiar symbol on the key to my sleuth?"

"Given your sister's actions, do you think that's wise?"

"It is my belief that she acted alone. And I wasn't going to send the entire thing, just an enlarged portion of that one bit."

"I guess that would be fine." She wouldn't get answers if she played her cards too close to the chest.

"You can trust me, Honeybear."

She snorted. "Don't make a promise you might not be able to keep."

"If I give you my word, I won't break it."

"How about promising to not kiss me again on some made-up pretext?"

"First off, I was maintaining our cover because someone was spying. And second, I can't promise that because kissing you was much too enjoyable."

"What if I don't want to be kissed?"

"I think you do."

He was right, but that didn't make her happy. She didn't want to want to kiss him. It didn't help that she craved another.

"No more kisses."

"What about fondling?"

"No touching, either."

"What if you climb on top of me again in your sleep?"

"How about you stay out of my bed?"

"I can't promise that. You might need a snuggle if you have another nightmare."

She might have argued more, but they'd reached the mall. "We're here." And she might have sounded a tad more ominous than necessary as she said, "Let's shop."

CHAPTER FIVE

The mall proved massive, two stories with a parking lot jammed with cars. She chose a spot in plain view of pedestrians, making it less likely for the vehicle to get broken into.

Once inside, she didn't get distracted by the purse store, or the jewelry one. She took Andrei straight to a popular chain of men's clothing. All much too small.

He shook his head. "I need something that offers real men's sizes, not this puny stuff." He held up a shirt that wouldn't have a seam left if he tried it on.

"Hmmm." She chewed her lower lip as she thought, making him jealous.

When he'd kissed her earlier, he'd done it because someone had followed them and was watching. But just one touch, and he'd not wanted to stop. Kissing her enflamed the senses. Made his inner bear rumble. Something inside him clicked, and he knew he was in trouble.

As she perused the mall's map, he couldn't help but ponder what it meant. Was this lioness his mate? He almost winced to think it, already knowing that his mother wouldn't like it. Fuck like. She'd outright reject Hollie on species alone.

Perhaps he was wrong.

"Let's try the Big and Tall store," she said, glancing at him over her shoulder. "They deal in above-average men."

"Glad to see you recognize my magnificence."

She snorted. "That would require less back hair."

"Don't disparage my lush pelt. You don't see me saying anything about your mustache."

Her hand went to her upper lip, but she couldn't completely hide her scowl. "Leave my fuzz alone."

"I like your fuzz."

"Hmph." She stalked off, angry at him. Yet that didn't stop her from halting abruptly and snapping, "You coming?"

He had a funny feeling he'd follow her anywhere. "Aye, *moy kapitan*," he said, giving her a salute.

She rolled her eyes, but her lips lilted in amusement. "Idiot."

Walking behind her didn't just mean watching that fine ass again. It also meant watching the people in the concourse. Did any of them pay too much attention to his honeybear?

He saw one human male who needed his eyeballs yanked out and squished for leering. Another actually started to approach her with a smarmy smile until

Andrei lengthened his stride and scowled in the man's direction.

During it all, she seemed oblivious, focused only on her destination. Or so he thought.

As he joined her outside the store, she muttered, "Way to blend in."

"Thank you.

"I was being sarcastic. What happened to being a master of disguise?"

"I thought I played the part of jealous boyfriend to perfection. Perhaps we should kiss again to make my performance complete."

Her gaze strayed to his mouth. Long enough that he knew she remembered the passion of it.

She abruptly turned. "Let's get this over with."

The establishment she located had true men's sizes. He grabbed an armful of things to try, with one admonishment once he realized that they both wouldn't fit in the cubicle.

"Stay in sight of the changing room."

She sighed. "Seriously? We're in a public place. A human mall, I might add. No one is going to try anything here."

"Those are the exact things that make it a perfect ambush spot because the enemy will expect you to let your guard down."

"You're being ridiculous."

"Don't make me leave the door open while I try on the clothes."

"Do it, and you'll get arrested for indecent exposure."

"Hollie!" He used her name for once in his sternest voice, and she grinned.

"Yes, Papa Bear."

He couldn't help but laugh. "I'm serious. Stay close," he exclaimed before shutting himself inside. He quickly began flipping things on and off, creating two piles.

He was down to his boxers, trying on the last pair of jeans when she said, "I think someone is watching me."

"Because you're hot," he said, slotting his feet into the legs. He opened the door, barefoot with the jeans not fully buttoned. He was gratified to see her staring. Swallowing. Before her gaze, bright with interest, met his. "Where?"

"Over by the sunglasses cart, outside the store. It's probably just a pervert."

"Or a guy with good taste." He glanced over her head and saw the man. His gaze narrowed. "It's the same person who was watching us at the university."

The fellow caught him staring, stiffened, and ran.

And his honeybear, with a hunter's instinct, took off after him, shouting over her shoulder, "Meet you at the van."

Like fuck. Immediately, he followed, only to have someone grab his arm. He looked down at the store clerk.

"Where do you think you're going? You have to pay for those pants!"

He glanced down at himself. Pay, or strip. He knew what Hollie would say. But his instinct screamed for him to do something. The pants hit the floor, leaving him in the boxers he'd tried on, also bearing a dangling tag.

He had no problem going naked, but he wouldn't be able to help if local authorities arrived and arrested him for theft or indecent exposure.

"Fuck." He whirled for the changing room, threw on his old jeans and shirt, then added his shoes, too. On the way out, he tossed his credit card and the clothes he'd chosen at the fellow. "Ring this up. I'll be back." And, yes, he said that in a *Terminator* voice. His mother had had him and his sister watching American movies from a young age to minimize their accent. Because, as she explained—sometimes with a wooden spoon—the more languages they knew, the better they could fit in. And ensure that no one took advantage of them.

While the clerk rang up the items, he took off in the direction he'd seen Hollie fleeing. He didn't need to see her to follow her scent. Hell, he wasn't even sure it was a sense of smell that drew him. It was simply instinct. As if he knew where to find her.

He caught up to her in one of the service corridors, her arm pressed over a man's throat. A human, not a shifter.

"What happened to not moving out of sight?" he barked, relieved that she appeared uninjured.

"Calm yourself, Papa Bear. As you can see, I have things in hand. You're just in time to hear some answers. Starting with, why are you following me?" She added a glare to the query.

The fellow stammered. "I wasn't."

"You were at the university."

"I'm a student there."

"Who just happened to end up at the mall where I did?" She arched a brow.

"I work here when I don't have classes." The reply was high-pitched and frightened.

"If that's the case, why did you run?"

"Because your boyfriend looked mad." The human's gaze shifted to Andrei, who smiled. A terrible grin that made the guy swallow hard.

"Why were you looking at me in the first place? Huh?" she snarled.

"Because you're pretty?"

"He has a point," Andrei stated.

"I think you're lying." She leaned in harder, and the fellow whimpered.

"I'm sorry. I promise I'll never look at you again." Even now, the guy couldn't face her. Fear rolled off of him, along with the thick stench of cowardice.

"You shouldn't eye women like they're meat. Ever. It's rude," she growled.

"I promise!" was the breathy agreement.

"I think you can let the little man go. He's learned

his lesson." Andrei let her believe that she'd threatened him into complacence. No need for her to know that he'd mimed throttling and slitting a throat behind her back.

She grunted as she shoved away from the guy, who scurried to the exit at the end of the corridor. She planted her hands on her hips as she said, "I didn't need your help."

"Obviously."

"I can handle myself."

"And you handled that ogler, too. Bravo."

She pursed her lips.

He did his best to not crack a smile.

"What happened to the clothes you were trying on?"

"Getting rung up. Can we fetch them or would you like to terrorize some more humans first?"

"Me? You're the one who glared him into running."

"And you just had to chase," he remarked as they headed back to the store to gather his large purchase.

"It's in my blood. I can't always help myself," she admitted.

"A natural hunter, and yet you chose plumbing?"

"My mom was a hunter for the Pride. A good one, too. She spent a lot of time away from home on jobs." Her shoulders lifted and fell. "I didn't want the same kind of life."

Left unsaid was the fact that a young girl felt lonely with her mother often gone.

He placed his arm over her shoulders and hugged

her to his side. "You should have been a bear. We don't like to wander far or for long."

"No one wants to be a bear." She ducked out of his embrace. "They're big, smelly, and hairy."

"True, but at least we don't lick our own asses."

She glanced at him, startled, and then she laughed.

The sound was like music, her genuine smile better than a patch of sunshine. Her good humor lasted until they reached her house and walked in to see that it had been vandalized.

CHAPTER SIX

T he violation left her speechless.

The demolition of Hollie's home wasn't just contained to a single room. It started in the front hall with her closet emptied of coats and footwear. It moved into the living room, where stuffing from the torn couch layered the floor in fluff. The pictures had been yanked from the walls, and holes were punched into the plaster. Not a single piece of furniture remained upright. In the case of the side table, the drawer wasn't just ripped out, it was splintered. Her kitchen was a mess of glass and spilled food.

The utter destruction appalled. And for what?

Not robbery, because valuables like her television were smashed not stolen. Her sparse jewelry, scattered.

"They were looking for something. And I'll bet I know what," was Andrei's grim observation.

"The key." Which she'd not left at home. Whoever

had tossed the place must have thought she'd hidden it before leaving, and obviously didn't believe that her aunts had it.

Andrei crouched, one hand gripping the floor as he leaned down and sniffed. "Three of them. Human. Two males. One female."

"Basic info that doesn't help us much." She didn't add the extra details she'd discerned, such as the fact that one of the men had eaten bacon that morning, or that the woman's shoe had spearmint-flavored gum stuck to the sole.

She concentrated more on the invasion of her home. Her space. All over a stupid key.

Her lips pursed. "In retrospect, I believe that guy at the mall was watching us."

"And relaying our location to whoever was searching," Andrei agreed. "But how did they know you even had it? The plan was for your aunts to pretend to have it in their possession and lead anyone looking for it on a merry chase. Would they have told anyone you had it?"

She shook her head.

"And given we only started searching today..." He trailed off, and she saw where he was going.

"You think Ted blabbed."

"He's the only one we talked to."

"I told him I didn't have it."

"Could be he didn't believe you."

"He wouldn't sell me out to humans," she stated, and yet it had been years since they'd dated. And, truthfully, he'd not proven himself trustworthy at that time given he cheated.

"Some people will sell their own family for the right price."

"I wouldn't," she emphatically stated.

"Because you're not an asshole," was his stark reply.

Not funny, and yet, she laughed—a low, bitter sound. "It's going to take me days, maybe even weeks to replace and repair this stuff." Where would she find another free pie plate table? She'd scrounged this one from a garbage heap, then sanded and repainted it. What of the couch? Bought at a liquidation sale.

All the things she'd worked so hard for. Gone. Tears pricked her eyes, and she turned, lest he see.

Not quickly enough.

"Oh, Honeybear. Don't cry."

"I'm not crying," she said in a thick voice. "I'm pissed."

"As you should be. This is someone being a dick. But, it can all be fixed. I promise. And more quickly than you think. We'll hire help."

"There is no *we*. This is my problem."

"You seem to have forgotten that I am a part of this."

"No, you're not. This is my home. My life. Fixing this is more important to me than an old key that's driving people to act batshit crazy."

"It's precisely because it's making people do desperate things that we need to find out what it is."

"Or they'll keep coming back," was her dull reply. The other solution was to hand off the key, which meant giving the problem to someone else. Running away like a coward. She rubbed at her stinging eyes. "Argh."

"Would you like to hit me to relieve some frustration?"

She eyed him. She wanted to hit him, all right, just not with her fists. "I'm not mad at you."

"What they did was shitty. Use that anger to focus on our next step. While we're working on figuring out what that key is, and who wants it, we'll hire some pros to fix this place."

"Says the guy with money. Not all of us are rich."

"I can help."

"I don't accept charity."

"Then consider it payment for your hospitality."

"You spent one night as my guest—and a day as an interloper."

"If you won't let me help, then will you accept a loan?"

"With what kind of interest and repayment terms?"

"Pay it back as you like, with the only interest being a kiss a day."

There was something heady about him making that demand. At the same time, Hollie took offense. "I am not paying you in sex."

"I would never dream of asking. But, a kiss? It takes

but a simple second to press your lips to any part of my body."

"So, I could kiss your hand?"

"Nose. Cheek. Or...other parts." The grin he flashed had more than a hint of naughty in it.

The offer was tempting because she had enjoyed their fake kiss. Andrei must have too, or he wouldn't be asking.

Still...she wasn't a whore who traded favors for money. She shook her head. "Your offer is generous, but I can't say yes."

"Understandable, if disappointing. In that case, would you accept my help in cleaning up some of the worst parts?"

Don't cut off your nose to spite your face. She could almost hear aunt Lena saying it. Meaning, don't let her pride turn her stupid. She nodded, and they spent the rest of that afternoon filling up trash bags. So many bags that she wasn't too mad when a dumpster arrived and was parked in her driveway. She had too much to simply put on the curb.

It took hours, but by the time they were done, her house was mostly empty and clean. A few things had survived. The kitchen chairs and table. Plastic dishes. Some clothes. But her mattress had been slashed.

She didn't need his frowned observation to realize the obvious. "We can't stay here tonight."

"I can probably stay with one of my aunts or in the guest suite at the Pride condominium until I can at least replace my bed." Which, in turn, meant letting the aunts know what had happened. They'd lose their shit. Still, they needed to know that someone was already coming after the key.

"If you don't want to impose on them, we could rent a hotel room," he suggested.

Her lips pursed. "You can. I have other options."

"That'd better include me. Now that you've been attacked, I am not leaving you alone for a moment, Honeybear."

"Would you stop calling me that? My name is Hollie."

"But you smell like honey."

"Then shouldn't it be Honeylion?" She arched a brow.

"Too late. It doesn't have the same ring. Besides, you're already Honeybear in my mind."

"How can it be too late? We met only a day ago."

"Yet, it feels as if I've known you longer."

Funny that he said it because it *did* feel that way. "Maybe you should find a new partner."

"I like the one I have. Besides, aren't you the least bit curious as to why they're so desperate?"

"More like pissed."

"Good. Don't let these assholes get away with ransacking your house. Shouldn't they be the ones paying to fix it?"

He did have a point. Still, she wasn't usually prone to revenge. Or psycho fits. She left that to those who called themselves the Baddest Biatches. She was just Hollie. Safe. Boring. Steadfast.

Her gaze caught the hole in the wall. They'd punched through the plaster, even though it was obvious that she couldn't have hidden anything inside. How dare they?

"Even if I wanted to go after the humans who did this, I don't know where to start." Because their trail ended at the curb where they clearly got into a car.

"I think it's time we visited this Peter fellow."

"You heard my aunts; we're not allowed to torture him for info."

"Who said anything about torture? There's more than one way to get information." He winked.

"Oh, hell no. I am not seducing the guy."

He snorted. "As if I'd agree to you touching another man. I've got a better plan."

"I'm afraid to ask what it is."

"Trust me, it will work."

Trust a big and brash bear? "You are incorrigible."

"But handsome, right?"

She shook her head, unable to completely stop the smile on her lips. "Yes, and a handful. I pity the woman who decides to try and tame you."

"Two handfuls, actually. And why would you want to tame me?"

Why, indeed. There was something about his wild personality that drew her. That made her want to be the less cautious one. One who took off after someone on the spur of the moment like today. One who got her blood pumping.

"What's the plan?" she asked.

Given a direct confrontation would probably get a door slammed in their face, and the Pride involved, Andrei suggested that they keep an eye on Peter's apartment building. In her van, which held an unseemly amount of fast food and drinks. Apparently, a stakeout required it.

But their watching paid off. A man fitting Peter's description eventually left the building, heading at a brisk pace down the street to a pub.

"He's being followed," Andrei noted, seeing the shadow that detached and kept a discreet distance.

She squinted. "I know that woman," Hollie said with a hint of surprise. "Kind of. We've never met in person, but I've seen her around. She recently began working for the Pride's security firm. Do you think she was hired to protect Peter?"

"Seems most likely. Either that or keep an eye on him."

"Regardless, we can't go near. If she sees us, she'll tattle."

"And say what? That we happened to run into Peter in a bar and shared some drinks. Surely, that's allowed."

"When you say drinks…"

There was that naughty grin again. "You said no torture. But what if a certain human got drunk and let some things slip?"

"Because he's going to want to get drunk with a stranger and spill his guts."

He snorted. "Do you not know men at all? We hate drinking alone."

"What about his shadow?"

"She'll be your problem."

"I am not knocking her out!"

He rolled his eyes. "And people say bears are quick to violence. Never said harm the woman. Just distract her. Buy her a beer."

"I don't drink."

"Then share some food. You're both from the same Pride. Surely, you can fake a friendly conversation for the greater good."

She stared at him. "It won't work."

"Why not?"

"Because I'm not a friendly person." Unlike most of the Pride, she avoided gatherings whenever possible. Didn't go out of her way to hang with people.

"Don't be silly, Honeybear. You have a delightful personality."

"I didn't take you for a liar."

He laughed, the sound too loud and boisterous for her van. Yet she strangely enjoyed it. "You have a most excellent sense of humor."

"It's called sarcasm."

"And some of us enjoy it." He tilted her chin with a finger and stared at her. His lips curved subtly. "You are special, Honeybear."

The compliment warmed her. But it didn't last long as Andrei opened the door on his side, and the van creaked as he spilled out.

"This is such a bad idea," she grumbled.

"Only if it doesn't work. I'll go in first. Wait a few minutes before you follow."

She leaned against her vehicle as he went up the street, sauntering without a care, a big and sturdy, fearless man, who made her feel the strangest things.

And she didn't just mean desire.

He saw something in her. Just like she was beginning to realize that there was more to him than just the brash bear. He was kind. Thoughtful. Flirtatious.

He probably acted like that with all the women. She wasn't special. Yet she was tempted to give in. To see what it would be like, if even only for a moment, to be swept up in the wild passion he promised.

To not be ready, steady Hollie.

Minutes passed, and Andrei didn't emerge. Neither did Peter or his shadow.

Taking a deep breath, she sauntered for the bar. She entered the human establishment, immediately bombarded by the smell of beer—old and new—fried food, and people.

A whole bunch of people this time of night, which had her glancing around. Not seeing a free table but spotting someone she knew seemed natural.

She settled her gaze on Peter's shadow and smiled as she approached. "Hey, what are you doing in this part of town?"

The woman's gaze flicked to her, and she frowned. "Um, eating. You?"

"Same. I just finished a plumbing job down the

street." She sat down. "I don't think we've officially met before. I'm Hollie."

"Nora."

And just like that, she faked being friendly.

It wasn't as hard as she'd expected. She could only hope that Andrei was having the same kind of luck.

CHAPTER SEVEN

Lucky Worm. The label on the bottle of tequila, almost empty now, that sat in front of him and his new friend Peter.

"You've never left the country at all?" Andrei questioned. He'd been slyly slipping queries into the conversation, trying to get Peter to spill his guts.

Since the man didn't have a loose tongue, evisceration and showing him his intestines were starting to sound good. Andrei was getting nowhere.

"I've been here and there across the States, but never had the time or inclination to go elsewhere."

Screaming, *"you're a liar"* would let the cat out of the bag. Revealed that Andrei knew more than he should about Peter. That this wasn't a chance encounter.

Had Peter already guessed that?

He seemed genuine. Likeable. Believable. But Andrei knew the truth. The human lied like a pro.

"You into antiques?" Andrei asked bluntly.

"Nah. I like my stuff new." Peter wrinkled his nose as he poured them another shot. No salt. No lime. It tasted like warm piss, and oddly wasn't the worst thing Andrei had ever drunk. Uncle Yogi's moonshine? Now that was some hardcore shit.

"I like old things. Collect a few, too. Got a sixty-seven Barracuda. Some antique desk with this puzzle drawer I can't figure out. It needs a key, I think, but it's long gone. And my mother won't let me take an ax to the thing."

"Hire a locksmith. They can pick it and then manufacture another key if you decide to keep it. Drink?" Peter nudged the glass, and Andrei wanted to sigh. He grabbed it and half turned to lean on the bar, his gaze straying to the back of Hollie's head.

He couldn't seem to help but check on her. He tossed back the shot of pee. Ugh. It sloshed in his belly. Mental note to self: next time, buy a bottle of Schnapps. It was harder to fuck up and didn't leave as bad of a taste if it came back up.

And this would be exiting his stomach shortly. Better now, through one end, than tomorrow, burning through the other. Even his shifter side didn't want to metabolize this crap.

"I'll be right back. Gotta break the seal."

He got back to see his shot glass refilled, and Peter watching the crowd in the bar, his gaze affixed on the table with Hollie and Peter's shadow.

"You married?" Peter asked as Andrei sat back on the stool beside him.

"Nope."

"I almost got married once. I escaped just in time."

"I wouldn't mind settling down." He wondered what had made Hollie laugh as her body shook. He could swear he heard it.

"I'm a wanderer."

"Didn't you say before you never left the country?" Aha, his plan to get the human drunk was working. He was the one to lift the shot glass first. "You should come to Russia."

"Is that where you're from?"

"*Da*. Born and raised."

"And why are you here?"

"I am a mail-order groom. Boyfriend, actually. Met a girl online. Came out here to spend time."

Peter eyed him and snorted. "As if."

"You don't think I'm handsome enough to be chosen?" He tossed back his drink. Poured another.

"I think it's very unlikely that's true."

"You're right. I lied. I'm actually a Soviet spy, here looking for a man who has information about a hidden treasure."

"A spy who's in a bar, getting drunk with me? Try again."

"Computer programmer, brought over from my country to hack your elections."

"Ha. Funniest one yet. Another shot?" Peter

poured but turned away before drinking, glancing at the women again.

Andrei nudged his new friend. "You should go over and say hello."

"They seem busy. And the one in the black shirt looks like she could kick my ass."

Wait, Hollie's shirt wasn't black. "She's pretty."

"Then maybe you should be my wingman and handle her while I go after the other one."

"You can't."

"Why not? You know her?"

"No." Said too hotly, so Andrei added, "But I'd like to. Therefore, you can't."

"Another?" Peter turned back to the bar to pour the shot while he kept his eye on Hollie.

The thought of another man flirting with her didn't sit well. Andrei grabbed the offered shot and downed it.

Grimaced. Blinked. The piss was getting to him. Maybe he should revisit the bathroom.

"What do you do for a living?" Peter asked.

"Deliver groceries." The most straightforward explanation.

Peter scoffed. "Way to aim high in life, big guy."

The human misunderstood, and Andrei didn't care enough to correct him. "What is your job?"

"A little bit of this and that. More of an entrepreneur, you could say. Shall we have another?"

There was no ball-saving way to say no. So, they drank until Andrei noticed that he was having a hard time focusing. Good thing he leaned on the bar because his balance appeared a bit off.

The shot glasses lined up in front of him wavered and split into two, and his new friend Peter said, "What shall we toast next?"

"Women," Andrei slurred. Even as only one actually filled his thoughts.

He and Peter knocked glasses and tossed them back. For a human, Peter was doing well. Better than Andrei.

The interrogation wasn't going so well. No matter how Andrei tried, Peter kept lying. Lied about ever being to Russia. Claimed he was an only child.

So, they drank some more. And still, Peter didn't slip.

Perhaps a visit to a nearby alley was in order.

If Andrei could stand up straight.

He just about face-planted when Peter slapped him on the back and said, "It's been fun, but I've got to get to bed. Early morning planned."

"Bye, friend." He pivoted to watch Peter exiting the tavern without the slightest sway to his step, his shadow soon following. A moment later, Hollie joined him at the bar.

"So?" she hissed. "What did you find out?"

"You're beautiful." The amount of tequila sloshing in his system had his words emerging with a hint of the accent he usually controlled.

"You're drunk."

"But not blind," he countered.

"Let's get out of here. I think you could use some fresh air."

"I am not drunk," he slurred as he tried to stand, and the room tilted. Obviously, an asteroid had hit the Earth and rocked it. He kept his balance, but Hollie obviously worried about falling over because she tucked against him and slid her arm around his waist.

They made it to the door and then had to separate to get through. Outside, the sidewalk rocked as if they were on a boat.

"Are we sailing?" he asked.

"Nope. Come on, the van is just down the street."

He took a step, and the world tilted again.

"Whoa." He waved his arms to keep his balance.

"Seriously?" she muttered as she snuggled under his arm again, obviously perturbed by the Earth's odd rocking. Because a big, strong bear did not need help walking.

See? He could walk just fine. One foot in front of the...okay, maybe sideways, but still going forward.

Oops. Who put that pole in front of him? She yanked him around, and they kept moving despite the swaying ground.

"Did you find out anything?" she asked.

"I found out American booze is stronger than expected."

"Because you drank way too much, idiot."

"It was his fault," he protested thickly. "He kept pouring shots."

"And you kept drinking them."

"Didn't want to be rude."

"Did he tell you anything about the key?"

"No. He acted like he was a simple human, out for a drink. He even lied about ever leaving the country." Said with a heavy growl on the consonants.

"Could be he forgot about it. The aunts said he was lost for six months and came back with no memory."

"Convenient," Andrei declared.

"Very. However, the fact he remembers nothing means we've hit another dead end."

"I'm not giving up!" he declared.

"Watch your step, almost there."

A glance showed two identical vans parked on the street. Had she franchised while he questioned Peter?

As they neared, she said, "Where do you want to go?"

"Bed."

"Obviously. Where, though?"

"With you."

"My bed is wrecked, remember? And it's kind of late to be knocking on anyone's door." She sighed. "Guess we should have figured this out before you got drunk."

"Not drunk. Only a little tipsy." The curb was a lot higher than expected, and he went reeling, stopped by the bumper of her van. He sat on it, and the whole thing groaned.

"I guess we could go to a motel."

"Yes." Motels had beds, and he needed one. He was having a hard time keeping his eyes open, which proved worrisome. He'd never been this wasted before, and he'd drunk more. He knew for a fact that American booze wasn't as potent as the stuff served in his home country. So why the spinning?

As she opened the back and admonished him to get in, he tried to focus. This was wrong. So wrong. The back of her van was crowded, but he made himself a spot and collapsed.

He vaguely heard her as she got into the driver's seat and mumbled something about him not being able to hold his liquor.

Again. Something about it didn't seem right. His stomach churned. Uh-oh. He did an unmanly thing and found a bucket.

The subsequent violent hurling resulted in the van lurching to a halt, which didn't improve his spinning head.

The harangue started. "Holy shit, puke outside! Don't you dare throw up on my tools. What the...?" She paused mid-sentence. "Someone just parked behind us. I think they're coming to see if we're okay. I better go deal with them."

She got out of the van, and despite his spinning head and rumbling belly, Andrei reeled on his haunches.

Danger.

Danger.

He felt like Will Robinson with that repeating message.

He could hear the murmur of his honeybear's voice

as she spoke to someone. Then the terseness of it as she got annoyed. Then the thump of something hitting the van.

Did someone dare to hit his honeybear?

Rawr!

There was no conscious thought, just action as he burst from the back of the truck on four paws.

His blurry vision noticed two men, or was it three, confronting Hollie. They gaped at his magnificence, then turned and ran screaming as he growled and then charged.

It might have been more impressive if his drunken ass didn't get tangled and land on his snout.

The humans got away, and his honeybear crouched beside him with a sigh.

"You big, dumb idiot. Let's get you somewhere safe."

With him obeying her soft voice, he ended up back in the van. A short time later, he was in a bed.

Dreaming of honey. Licking and lapping and happy as could be.

Ignoring the buzzing and whirring of bees. Poking him. Pricking him. Swirling to form shapes.

A specific shape.

The configuration familiar.

Why was it familiar?

It hit him, and he sat up in bed and shouted, "I know where I saw it!"

CHAPTER EIGHT

The yell had Hollie bolting from her bed, brandishing a wrench, ready to fight only to see that her giant bear had woken as a spiky-haired, wild-eyed, naked man.

"Now, who's having nightmares?" she grumbled, dropping back onto the pillow that smelled strongly of bleach.

"Not a nightmare, but a vision. I know where I saw that symbol on the key."

"Which one?" she asked, realizing that sleep wouldn't be forthcoming. She sat back up and propped herself against the headboard.

"I'll show you. Where is it?"

"Hiding." And she wasn't telling anyone where.

"Show me the picture, then."

She rolled over and palmed her phone, unlocking it to access the gallery before reaching out to hand it over.

Instead of grabbing it, he stood, much too close with his naked, hanging parts, and began making a happy growly noise. "Yes, there it is." He shoved the phone at her. "You see that line here and here." He jabbed the screen. She yawned.

"Sure. What of it?"

"I've seen it before. In a book I had as a child."

Now he had her attention. "What was the name of the book?"

He frowned. "I don't know. My nanny used to read it to me."

"So call her and ask for the title."

"I can't. She's long gone, and I don't know where. I remember my mother grumbling about how much she paid to employ her. She was quite efficient, acting as nanny and tutor in one until we got old enough to go to school."

"Doesn't matter how long she was with you. We only need her name."

"Nanny."

"Her actual name."

He shrugged. "I was young. I called her Nanny."

"Well, that's kind of useless. Do you remember the story? Maybe I can find it via an internet search."

That brought another crease to his brow as he sat on the edge of the bed. "It was a long time ago. It had something to do with a quest. As a boy, I found it boring because it lacked war and violence. But my sister,"—he paused—"she used to love it."

Finally, a real clue. "We need to find that nanny."

"She could be anywhere, though."

"And? Doesn't matter where she is, we have to pay her a visit. We just need her name and some basic info to locate her."

"I told you, I don't know her name."

"Ask your mother. She probably remembers."

That brought a vigorous shake. "No. We can't call her."

"Why not?"

"She's not happy I left Russia."

"But you did it for a good reason."

"We cannot call." Stated quite firmly.

"Then how else will you get your nanny's information?"

He pursed his lips. "What you ask of me is impossible. We will find another way. Perhaps I'll have a dream with her name."

Was Andrei really that scared to call his mother?

What if Hollie bribed him?

"I will give you a kiss if you do it."

"Really?" His expression brightened, then sobered. "As much as I am tempted. I must say no."

"A long kiss. With tongue."

"Argh. Why must you torture me, Honeybear?" He paced the narrow space between the queen-sized beds. Torturing her with all that naked flesh.

"Have a shower and think about it."

"I need food." He scrubbed a hand through his hair.

"For that, you'll need clothes." Thankfully, she'd

managed to salvage some of her clothes from her place, despite it being wrecked. And his had never made it out of the store bag.

She pointed to the pile on the table by the window.

"Why am I naked?" he asked as if realizing it for the first time. "And how did we get here?"

"You got drunk with Peter last night."

"Impossible."

"Says the guy who was passed out in my van one minute, puking the next, and then finally going wild bear on a rampage."

"I shifted?" His brows almost rose off his forehead.

"Yup. I'm just hoping no one got any videos of your hairy ass."

"That shouldn't have happened." He appeared almost embarrassed.

"You were drunk out of your mind."

"Which makes no sense. I've been drinking since I was this tall." He held his hand to a spot that would indicate a young age. "I was weaned on vodka. Have been on binges that lasted days and never blacked out."

She frowned. She had thought it odd he'd been so drunk, and quickly too. "You think you were drugged? But how? By who?"

"Peter," he grumbled.

Had to be, which meant the man obviously realized that Andrei had been questioning him. "I think we need to have another chat with the man."

"Yes." Andrei slammed a fist into his palm. "After breakfast."

"And a shower." She wrinkled her nose at him.

"Shall we conserve water and take one together?" was his hopeful request.

"I highly doubt we'd both fit." Which wasn't a no she realized a second too late as he smiled widely.

"We could try."

She shook her head. "Not happening, puke breath."

The reminder brought a glower and a stomp as he hit the bathroom. A good thing, too, because that much naked Andrei wreaked havoc on her senses. She was half-tempted to join him and soap his back. Then his front. Then who knew where that would lead...

She eyed the mussed bed.

They really shouldn't, even as she had a feeling it was only a matter of time before it happened.

While he showered, she checked in with Aunt Lacey. She had texted them her location the night before, knowing they would get worried if she didn't. While they didn't hover over her as badly as they did their nephew/son Lawrence, she had been the recipient of more than one well-meaning auntie visit.

Aunt Lacey answered. "Hollie, how was your night?"

"Fine."

"Only fine with that hunk of a man?" Lacey teased.

"Before you get all excited, nothing happened. It's possible Andrei was drugged."

"What? By who? When? How?"

"Peter."

"You better tell me what happened."

Hollie quickly explained, and Lacey grew quiet. "I'm beginning to think we're going to have to go against Lawrence on this and question that boy. He's lying to us."

"Obviously."

"I'll relay what you told me to Lena. She'll know how to handle it."

"Maybe you should get someone else to take over the key, too. I haven't been doing a very good job with it so far." Which disappointed. For a woman who'd not wanted this stupid quest, she now felt discouraged at her failure.

"Did you think it would be easy?"

"No, but the only clue we've gotten is something about Andrei's old nanny." Which then required more explanation.

"Hollie, how can you say you haven't done a good job when you're the first to actually start cracking the mystery?"

"I have?"

"You need to follow up on this book thing while we handle Peter and whoever broke into your house."

"But my job..."

"Will still be here when you're done. We need you handling this, Hollie."

"Why me? Why not one of the Baddest Biatches?" They usually handled Pride matters.

"Because we know we can trust you to not get your head turned around. Not to mention, you're the only one who appears able to work with Andrei without trying to make him into a rug."

She blinked. "You mean, I'm not the first person you've paired him with."

"Nobody else lasted an hour."

"Because he's crazy."

"He's a bear." As if that were the only explanation needed.

Hollie sighed. "You'll owe me big time for this."

"Would it help if I said I'm thinking of a bathroom reno?"

"Only if you don't expect a friends and family discount."

"That's my girl," was Lacey's fond reply. "Have fun."

Fun? She hung up the phone and eyed the bathroom door. She wanted to laugh at the absurdity of the statement. And yet, she *was* enjoying herself.

Especially when he emerged wearing only a small towel that he fisted by his hip to hold in place.

Moisture gleamed on his bare upper body.

She was suddenly very thirsty. Her gaze lifted to find him watching her. His expression smoldered, and she knew it would take only the slightest invitation for him to kiss her.

She licked her lips. He took a step towards her.

For once, she wished she was as bold as her cousins and the aunts. That she could throw herself at him and take a kiss. Because she wanted one.

"What's wrong, Honeybear?"

"Nothing."

"That expression didn't look like nothing. You seem confused."

"I am."

"I understand. It must be hard to be so attracted to me. I am, after all, quite the catch as you Americans would say. And yet, we are opposites. We don't even live in the same country. How would it work? Would we stay here? In Russia? Split our time?"

The more he spoke, the more she stared without blinking. "What?"

He'd gotten close enough that he could reach out and tip her chin. "Stop fighting your attraction to me. It's natural."

"Speaking of things that come naturally." She slugged him hard enough that he coughed. As he bent a bit, she smiled. "Thanks for reminding me you're conceited."

"Is it conceit if it's true?"

Her mouth rounded. The man was utterly shocking. But funny.

His lips curved, and she couldn't help but smile in return.

"You're screwing with me."

"Not yet, but I would like to. However, we don't have time. The people seeking the key will locate us. We should be gone before they do."

By the time they were both clean and ready to go, her stomach was growling. She'd gotten used to the massive amounts of food Andrei ordered and thus was shocked when he stuck to just one farmer's breakfast.

"You really must not be feeling well. Still hungover?"

He grunted.

The real reason for his malaise became apparent after breakfast when he looked at her with a pained expression and said, "I must call my mother."

"It won't be that bad."

"It will be worse," was his ominous prediction. The morose expression had her lifting on tiptoe to brush her lips across his. Quickly enough that he didn't have time to react other than to suck in a breath.

"Be a good bear and call. And if you get your nanny's name, there's another one coming."

"What do I get for an address?"

She winked.

She.

Winked.

What the hell was wrong with her that she also said, "Be a good bear, and you'll get a reward." Since when did she flirt and promise sexual favors?

Since she'd met a man that drove her nuts and wet her panties.

He should have been everything she hated. Yet she couldn't deny her intense attraction to him.

Please don't let it be anything else.

Mated to a bear? Never. Especially one as wild as Andrei. He'd never be tamed.

"I'll need to borrow your phone," he said.

"Don't you have one?"

"No. Too easy to track," was his ominous reply.

She handed it over, and, with a long-suffering sigh, he dialed then paced the parking lot, phone to his ear.

Someone must have answered because he said, "Hello." What followed was a stream of Russian—or so she assumed. She didn't catch a single word, but she watched his face. Apologetic. Eye rolling. Then excited. Followed by angry and finally shocked. "No. No. Fuck. No!"

He took the phone from his ear and eyed it as if it were evil.

"What's wrong? Did you get the information?"

"Yes."

"But?"

"My mother is worried."

"And?" she asked.

"My mother is what you might call overprotective." The phone in his hand rang. Insistently. But rather than answer, he tossed it to the ground and stomped on it.

"Dude!" she yelled. "What the hell? You just crushed my phone."

"I had no choice. I had to break the link. We must leave."

"But we don't even know where—"

"We'll figure it out on the way to the airport. If we move quickly, we should have a few hours head start."

"On who? Do you think someone was listening in on the conversation?"

"Worse," was his groaned reply. "My mother is coming."

CHAPTER NINE

This was about to get bad. So bad. Andrei could feel it in his bones. The hair on his back had probably turned white. With only himself to blame.

Any idiot could have guessed calling his mother wouldn't end well. His poor honeybear had no idea of the trouble that one phone call had started. The beast he'd unleashed.

"Where are you?" his mother barked the moment she answered. *Instinct let her know who was on the other end, even though she'd never seen the number before.*

"Hi, Mama." Spoken softly in Russian, along with an added, "Miss you. Love you. How's it going with the sleuth?" The best course of action at this point? Appear contrite and loving.

"Where are you?" she repeated. Not a good sign.

"In America. On business, as you well know." The

screaming match before their departure where she'd argued against his actions still rang in his ears.

"Where. Are. You?" An ominous repetition that had him scuffing the ground with his shoe.

"I'm okay. You don't need to worry."

"Where are you?" Mama hollered, starting to lose her shit.

He'd glanced at the sky. So pretty and blue. The sun doing its best to shove away the chill of the night. What he wouldn't give to be lying naked in a patch of warmth rather than having this conversation. "I am not telling you," he finally said.

Again, he knew better. Could have recited the following rant word for word. It didn't change much.

"Lying to your mother? The woman who birthed you. Loved you. Raised you when your wastrel of a father left." His father had left because his mother could be a bit much. It took a strong man, like Andrei, to love her.

Lada, on the other hand, could never find common footing. Unlike Andrei, she never gave in to their mother's demands. Perhaps the peacefulness of the house when she left was why Mama didn't look too hard.

His mother kept going. "I did homework with you every night."

"And you cooked and cleaned, kept house, went to work, cured cancer. Oops, wait, that's the only thing you haven't done." He couldn't help but poke the bear.

Mama retaliated by changing tactics. "Who drove

you to the hospital when you thought jumping off that cliff was a good idea?"

"How was I to know the water had evaporated that much?"

"The one who tended you during that fever?"

"No one told me honey could go bad."

"You don't think. It's why you need me."

His mother had wiped his ass and micromanaged his life for more than three decades. A good thing, or he'd have gotten into so much more trouble.

Andrei needed a firm hand to guide him. But maybe it didn't have to be Mama's.

He glanced at Hollie. She scowled at the sky as if offended that it dared to be nice outside. But when she glanced at him, her lips twitched. She arched a brow and mouthed, *"Mommy problems?"*

She had no idea.

His mother kept haranguing. *"Disrespecting me. Is this because of your American friends?"* An inflection on the word. *"Are they teaching you to disrespect the one person in your life who would never let you down. Who sacrificed. Who—"*

"Loves me. I know. Listen, before you start alphabetically listing all the ways I owe and need you, I have a question for you. Remember that woman who took care of me as a kid?"

"Why are you asking?"

"Because, now that you're almost sixty, all the experts say I am supposed to start testing your cognitive skills."

"Did you just call me old?" The shock could almost be grabbed.

"Are you avoiding the question because you don't know the answer?" he countered.

"Her name was Mila."

"Mila, what?" he cajoled. "Prove you aren't senile."

"Mila Miskouri, you little shit. Are you happy now?"

"Do you know where she lives?"

The last question changed the balance of power. He'd given away too much.

His mother's tone deepened ominously. "Why are you asking about your old nanny? Why the sudden interest?"

"No reason." The wrong answer, because his mother could always smell a lie.

"What is going on? Better yet, get your buttocks home."

"Relax and drink your hot chocolate."

"I am too anxious for chocolate."

"Since when has anxiety ever stopped you." His mother enjoyed a heaping plate of chocolate chip, soaked in her massive tankard of hot chocolate with the top frothed with marshmallows and whipped cream.

"I can't eat or sleep, I'm worried sick about you."

"If you're that ill, you should see a doctor."

"Why bother when I know he'll tell me it's a broken heart. I probably don't have long to live." She coughed pathetically.

It was a familiar game with his mother. First, the

straight demand that he spill his guts, then the listing of all the things he owed her, followed by the angry phase. Now, they were in the portion where she insisted that she was dying, and he didn't love her.

"Do you want to be cremated or buried in dirt?" Perhaps a touch too far in some families, but in his, where the drama ran high, kind of expected.

"Like a dagger to my heart," she exclaimed.

Before she went off again, he flipped the narrative on her. "If you missed me so much, you'd already be in America. Seeking me out and interrupting whatever I was doing." His mama was particularly gifted at showing up during his intimate moments with a partner, bearing a box of condoms. He appreciated the forethought—rubbers instead of diapers—but his partners didn't always react well.

"I want to be out there looking for you. But you know, it is a busy time for me. I can't drop everything and rush off to get you out of trouble."

"I could have been dead in a ditch." Yeah, he overdid it.

But so did Mama. "Then I would have avenged you."

He laughed. "Glad to hear it."

"How goes the groveling to make up for what your sister did?"

His mother was well aware that he'd come to the States to mend things with the Pride, given his sister's actions.

"It's not groveling. I'm helping them figure out why Lada acted as she did."

"Your sister always did make bad choices."

"How come you'll stop me from doing stupid shit but not her?" he asked.

"You're a boy. You need more help."

The double standard burned. Burned hot, which might be why he stupidly said, "Glad to hear you have such trust in those without a penis, because I'm working with a gorgeous woman. Like really remarkable. Smart. Pretty. Did I say amazing?" He couldn't stop his mouth from running. Was he still drunk?

The dead silence stretched.

Uh-oh.

His mother finally asked, "Who?"

"No one you've met." No one Mama could ever meet. She'd hate Hollie on sight. Before that. Out of sight. His mother never liked any of his girlfriends. He was pretty sure she might have gotten rid of one, too.

"Who?" his mother repeated.

His mind screamed at him to not say her name. At least not her real name.

He saw Hollie eyeing him, not understanding the Russian, but she probably hadn't missed his horrified expression.

He babbled, "I need to go now."

"Who?" The single syllable vibrated, and he clenched his teeth against the demand...

"Talk to you tomorrow?" was his high-pitched query.

"Area code five five five. Not bear county. Isn't that for lions?"

"Really? I wouldn't know."

"I should hope you aren't consorting with felines."

He eyed Hollie, who looked ravishing in worn blue jeans, a shirt with Mario on it, and a worn plaid jacket. His mama would never approve.

That wouldn't stop him.

"Look at that," his mother mused aloud. *"According to the Google, the phone number you're calling from belongs to a business. Owned by a Hollie Joliette. A plumber? That's unexpected."*

Oh.

Fuck.

"I borrowed the phone," was his hasty rebuttal. Too late.

"I can't wait to meet her," his mother said sweetly. Too sweetly.

"I don't think that's a good idea." Ever. His mother would probably go grizzly—which she got from her father's side—and Hollie would either threaten her with a wrench or tear a stripe. Then he'd get in the middle. Probably get hurt. Hollie would never want to see him again. And Mama would probably make him suffer for at least a week by making all his favorite foods but not letting him eat any.

"See you soon."

Suddenly desperate—and panicked—he hung up the phone. It rang. He stopped it.

As he stared at the wreckage of the phone and

explained to Hollie that they were fucked. She laughed.

"I don't believe this. You're afraid of your mother." Her words had an incredulous lilt to them.

"Everyone is. Especially the women I meet. We have to get out of the city," he stated, even as he feared there was nowhere he could hide.

"You're going overboard. Surely, she's not that bad."

How to explain? He'd only barely made it out of Russia, his mother having thrown a fit. He'd smuggled himself into a cargo hold to leave, and when he landed, had used a payphone to call and tell her that he was fine. She'd disowned him, so he hung up. He figured she'd calm down eventually. Past trips had more or less followed the same pattern. Although of late, she didn't always come after him. Maybe the fights when he left were only for show.

But he had a feeling this time would be different. He'd bragged about Hollie. What had possessed him to do such a thing? It was like waving a red blanket in front of his uncle Liam.

His mother knew that he wouldn't have mentioned Hollie unless she meant something to him. And his mama would never leave something like whom he mated to pure chance. Not with her perfect boy.

She would be coming. It was just a matter of when. If only his mother would extend that much effort to tracking down his troublesome sister.

"We need to get to an airport," he said, heading

into the hotel room, rounding up their things, and stuffing them into their bags.

"Wait, why are we flying? Where are we going? Did your mother give you a name and address?"

"Name, yes. Mila Miskouri. No address."

"But you assume she lives out of state."

"Given she was my nanny when I lived in Russia, I'd say the chances of her living in your town are slim to none."

"Good point." But Hollie still had questions. "Will they let me fly with just a driver's license?"

"Within the States, yes. But not if we leave them. If we do, we'll need your passport."

"Are they easy to get? Because I don't have one."

That froze him mid-action of stuffing his shirt into her knapsack. "How can you not have a passport at your age?"

Her shoulders rolled. "Never needed it since I've never left the country. We've discussed this."

"Well, it doesn't really matter, since I don't have one either." His mother had burned the last three when she found them.

"Do we need to get fake ones? Because I might know a gal who does them. Melly's pretty connected to that kind of stuff."

"We don't have time to wait. We'll just have to fly without a ticket."

"What about TSA and stuff? They're super strict now."

"Don't worry, I've got it mostly handled."

"That's what I'm afraid of," she muttered. Then she eyed him. "You actually called your mom to ask about your nanny. You've earned a kiss if you'd like one."

Did she seriously have to ask? "The thought of it is the only reason I called."

"Oh." She blushed. Tough girl with a mushy interior. Mmm.

She leaned up on tiptoe but needed a little help from him to press her mouth to his. A long kiss that left them both panting and flushed. It might have ended up with them naked if only a mental image of his mother getting on a plane to come here didn't douse him with icy reality. "Much as I'd like to do more of that, we need to finish packing and get moving."

"Get moving where? You have a name but no location yet."

"No, but with her name, we can find an address."

"How? You know, if someone hadn't destroyed my phone, we could have searched for your nanny online," his honeybear sassed.

"You could have warned me that you didn't have a private number."

"I'm a business. Of course, it's not private." She rolled her eyes.

"We will buy a new cell on the way to the airport."

"I haven't said I want to leave."

"If we're going to solve the mystery of the key, we must travel."

"Or we could, you know, call." She held extended

fingers to her mouth and ear and mimed talking into her curled digits. "Have you heard of this awesome invention called a telephone? You dial a number. The person picks up. You talk."

Calling meant staying here with his mama on the way. "We can't compare the image in the book to the key if we're not there in person."

"If she even still has the tome. How long ago was this?" she countered.

"The volume was already old when she read it to us, meaning it's probably a family heirloom. She would preserve it."

"She won't want strangers pawing it then. She could send us pictures."

"What if she doesn't have a camera or data?" he argued, unable to give her the real reason, which was that he wanted to spend more time with her. If they solved the mystery of the key too quickly, then he wouldn't have an excuse to be around her.

"We could buy another copy of the book."

"Why are you arguing so vehemently about going?"

"Because I don't understand the rush. Let's call first and make sure it's worth our while."

"We should get out of town for a bit until things settle down. Have you forgotten you were attacked?" The expression on her face when she beheld the damage to her home would haunt him for a while. What if she'd been there when it happened?

"Please. Admit you want us to leave quickly

because you think your mother is coming. Ooooh." She waggled her fingers. "Scary."

"Why are you being so ornery about going? Are you scared?" he taunted.

"No," she exclaimed.

"Then, let's just go."

"Just go." She snorted. "I highly doubt anything you do is so simple."

It was uncanny how well she understood him. And the trust she put in him because she *did* follow.

They were soon on their way, and true to his word, they stopped to buy a phone with a data plan. The only person who knew they were leaving was her family. She fired a group text to her aunts.

FYI the bear is taking me on a trip.

The reply? *Where?* They didn't ask who most likely because there weren't many bears hooked up with someone the aunts knew.

Not sure yet.

Egg or the chicken?

A car honked behind him as he got caught staring at her phone and not paying attention to the road.

"Why is your aunt texting you about eggs and chickens?" he asked.

"It's our system. Egg, or anything ova related, means alive and well. The chicken is, I'm in trouble because I can't fly."

"And what are you texting?"

Her lips twitched. "Salad."

"What's that supposed to symbolize?"

"Nothing. It will just drive them nuts a bit."

"You're close to your aunts?" he asked, taking his gaze from the road for a second.

"They were around more than my mom was. Which isn't saying much. I spent most of my youth in a boarding school."

"That's shit."

"It wasn't that bad. Then I was bounced between a bunch of the Pride's aunts as I became a teen. At sixteen, the old king let me have my own place."

"I still live at home."

"Please don't tell me in the basement."

"Our compound doesn't have one."

"You live in a hippie commune?"

"A sleuth, actually. The compound is a series of connected buildings and homes."

"But you live with your mom."

"Lots of bears do," was his defensive response.

"If you say so."

"I wouldn't talk. The Pride lives on top of one another in that condo you guys run."

"They do. I don't. Some of us like standing on our own two feet."

"Some of us let others hold on since their feet don't work as well."

"You're saying you stay home to support those unable to?"

"Yes, and because Mama does my laundry and cooks."

She stared at him, and he swore she almost laughed.

She kept it to a small smile as she said, "Speaking of your mom, she texted me."

"Impossible. I got you a burner. No one has your number."

"Not true. My aunts have it." And had apparently shared it. She held up the phone. It said simply: *Hands off.* "Would you like to reply?" she asked.

"No," he growled. This was new. His mother cock-blocking via text. "Block her."

"What if there's an emergency?"

"Rather than worry about my mother, we should be searching for my nanny's location."

"No mommy issues, my ass," she muttered as she went to work on searching.

At red lights, she showed him various pictures on Mila Miskouri's social media until he said, "Her. I think that's my nanny." Mila Miskouri had gotten older and grayer since she'd changed his diaper.

"According to the profile, your nanny retired two years ago at sixty-five and moved to South America."

"Meaning we have a destination. Here's hoping there's a flight going out today."

"Which does us no good since neither of us has a passport."

"I told you, we don't need them. Legal documents are for people who travel inside the cabin."

She stared at him. "Because that's how it's supposed to be done."

"I prefer the cargo hold."

"Isn't that packed tight with luggage?"

"Ever wonder why some of it never makes it to its destination?"

It took her only a second. "You stow away by throwing out people's stuff?"

"More like making room. You'll see, it's awesome."

"I highly doubt that," she muttered.

At the airport, he went inside but only so they could peek at the departure board. And what did Hollie do? Kept distracting him. He'd be reading something, and then, from the corner of his eye, she'd shift. He'd stop reading, then he'd get paranoid and start scanning the crowd.

She noticed. "Why do you keep jumping?"

"I'm being observant."

"Think your mother is already here?" she teased.

"Never know. She has spies everywhere." He didn't reveal his real reason for being so watchful. The humans who'd targeted her house. What if they came after Hollie next? His old pal Lawrence had gotten kidnapped and drugged by Lada and her crew. They'd taken Lawrence's human mate, too. Luckily, his good friend had escaped, even killed a few of his attackers in the process. But not all of them. Obviously. Hollie's destroyed house made it clear that someone was still after the key.

His honeybear was in danger, and this time, he wouldn't let her down.

He'd eat people first.

How he admired her; her character, strength, beauty. When she spoke, it was sarcastic and clever. Unique. Sexy.

Mate.

His other side seemed so sure of it. It would nibble her skin in a second and carry her off to a cave somewhere for some hibernating sexy times if allowed. The problem being, Andrei couldn't move too fast with Hollie or she'd retreat. Seduction had to go two ways, and while she kept giving indications that she might be interested, things kept getting in the way.

He saw her lips moving and took a second to blink and say, "What?"

"I said, did you find a flight? Because the only South American one I saw leaves in nine hours."

His mind went blank. The only thing he knew was that they couldn't wait here for nine hours. "I have a better idea. Hold on." He scanned destinations and marked the gate info of the one leaving the soonest.

"I still don't see how we are supposed to get into the cargo hold of a plane given all the security." Doubt hung thick in her statement.

"By being sneaky."

"Listen here, Papa Bear, master of disguise, you're well over six feet and built like a refrigerator. I don't know how you figure you can sneak on board."

"Watch and learn." He winked.

"I don't need to be taught how to be arrested."

"Only if we get caught. Which, we won't."

It started with him getting them through a door to

the bowels of the airport, which wasn't hard. It required accidentally bumping into an attendant and stealing their keycard, all without them raising the alarm. Then, they entered the employee locker room and broke into a storage room where they kept the spare uniforms.

Dressed like they belonged, they headed out, nodding at other workers. At least, he was. Hollie scowled, and her grumpy mien worked, too.

Andrei led them more by instinct than signage to gate thirteen and a flight to Mexico. From there, it would be easier to locate a plane traveling even farther south.

At the gate, he hustled to the luggage truck, just in time as the scheduled suitcase workers emerged.

Only one of them posed a half-hearted, "We're supposed to do thirteen."

"Apparently, not," Andrei drawled.

The other two workers shrugged and went back inside.

"This is way too easy," she said.

"People look for the suspicious. Those paying too much attention. Those that don't fit in."

"Just wearing a uniform shouldn't make it that simple."

"Longer scrutiny would shatter the disguise, but at a glance, you and I appear to belong here. It helps it's raining, and no one wants to be outside today."

"Hiding in plain sight," she remarked as he parked by the ass end of the plane, a section of it open to receive baggage. "If you're so good at it, why are we running from your mother?"

"More like going to find my nanny. And before you say once more that we could have called, I prefer the personal touch."

Her laughter exposed his bullshit, but she'd yet to walk away.

He climbed into the cargo end of the plane and arranged a proper nest for them. He had her tucked inside as he moved the little luggage truck then jogged back. He pretended to fiddle with something until more flight preparation crew moved out of sight, then he clambered in as the door began to close.

Despite the dark, he made his way to her side. She sat cross-legged and nervous, not that her tone betrayed it. "How cold is it gonna get?"

"Chilly enough that my back hair will come in useful."

She uttered a choked chuckle. "My fur isn't as warm as yours."

"Don't worry, Honeybear. I'm hot enough for both of us."

The plane hummed as it moved, and he felt more than saw her nervousness.

"Maybe I can find some clothes in the suitcases. I'll stay warm with enough layers."

"We could also stay warm joining the mile-high club," he suggested.

"I'm surprised you're not already a member," was her reply.

"Have you ever seen the size of those bathrooms on board?"

"You mean you don't always travel in baggage?"

"Only on rare occasions."

"Gee, feeling special now."

He laughed. "Would you have preferred being cramped inside the plane with shitty food?"

"Yes, and no. What if I get hungry?"

"I packed a snack."

"Wow, you're prepared. I'll bet your girlfriends love it when you take them on trips."

"You're the first I've smuggled with me."

She didn't say anything for a second. "I'm not your girlfriend."

"But I'd like you to be."

"Oh."

Silence.

He didn't push it. Instead, he pulled out the picnic lunch he'd brought. They ate by the glow of a dildo and an anal plug. She wore someone's sweater from another suitcase as she'd refused to touch anything in the one with all the sex toys.

"Who travels with that many batteries?" she'd exclaimed.

"Someone who isn't good with their hands."

She'd giggled, the sound fun and light. He'd reached for her and drew her close, meaning to kiss her, only to feel her shivering. She was cold.

"Time to change into our fur." Stripping didn't

take long, and then he shifted. He gave her his back as he knocked the sex toys aside and made some room.

A chuff from behind had him settling on his side before lifting a paw and beckoning.

A lioness with a sleek body of golden fur sat with her head cocked. Would she snuggle with him?

She dropped and pushed into him, her back against his chest, tucked into a ball with him wrapped around her.

And, yeah, he knew lions didn't purr. But for just a minute, he could have sworn she did.

CHAPTER TEN

Before landing in Mexico, Andrei ensured that they were dressed as tourists and not stowaways. A summer dress with sandals for her. Board shorts and a button-down Hawaiian for Andrei in a 3X that barely fit over his shoulders but had too much fabric in the belly. He'd had to keep wearing his loafers, though. None of the luggage had sandals in his size.

The moment they slipped out of the cargo hold, and after bribing the guy whose surprised face spotted them, they left the main terminal and entered a more industrial area for the airport at Hollie's behest.

"Where are you taking us?" he asked, tempering his stride to match her shorter one.

"You forget who my family is," she said, keeping an eye open for the hangar that Nora sent her via email. Because, wouldn't you know, over the course of the dinner at the bar, they'd played their cards straight and banded together to help each other. Mainly, Nora would let Hollie know if she discovered anything from Peter, and Hollie would repay the favor in kind, keeping her in the loop about attacks and the progress of the key.

"You told someone where we're going," he stated.

"I told a few people, actually." She ticked off her fingers. "My aunts so they'd know who to kill if I don't return. My king because he'd want to know. And Nora, who is currently my liaison back home. Since watching Peter isn't time-consuming, she's going to coordinate as much as she can from the ground."

"That's a lot of people." He grimaced.

"Would you feel better if I told you I didn't text your mom? Although, her latest message was interesting. Something about dying and taking you out of her will."

"Third time this year," he muttered.

"Your mother really is nuts."

"I told you."

For some reason, she grinned. "Your mommy lo-o-ov-es you," she sang.

"I'd be willing to share."

Her nose wrinkled. "No, thanks."

"So where exactly are we going? Did you manage to get us a private charter? With a sleeper cabin?" Said with such hope.

"That wouldn't be very discreet. We're riding on a Pride cargo plane." She'd messaged Nora from the luggage hold while he'd parked the cart at their departure airport. By the time they landed, Nora had already made the arrangements.

"As livestock?" he said as they passed a set of empty cages sitting outside a warehouse.

"Hell, no."

"It's a great cover if a tad uncomfortable after a few hours of not being able to stretch."

She did a double step and almost tripped. "You've been caged before?"

"Yeah. I don't recommend it. No room to stretch or do your business."

She bit her lower lip. "Dare I ask why?"

"Poachers kidnapping animals for private sport."

"You got caught?"

"On purpose. Then dismantled the operation from the inside."

She didn't need the details. His broad and somewhat evil grin said it all.

"I should have known you'd be the clichéd hero type."

"Not a hero. Those poachers were infringing on our territory. They served as an example of what happens when you cross a Medvedev."

"So, anti-hero, then."

"Also known as the villain," he declared.

"No, that would be your sister and the group she's working with."

"I don't want to be the hero." Said with an exaggerated pout.

"Don't worry, I'll steal all the glory solving this

mystery, and you'll just be the pretty face who carried my stuff." She patted his cheek and then left his side as she entered a hangar with a parked plane.

"You called me pretty," he crowed, his stride taking him past her.

"In a rugged, hairy way." Which was more and more appealing the more time they spent together.

"My heart. It is exploding with joy." He clutched his chest and grinned. "Perhaps later, I can make you explode with joy, too." He winked.

And there went her smooth replies and sarcastic comebacks. "That's our ride." Yup, she'd changed the subject. And he chuckled. A smooth, low sound that tickled over her, heightening her awareness.

The large repurposed aircraft didn't only deal in crates and supplies. It had a cozy passenger area, retro-fitted with patched couches that face each other, a fridge bungied in place, and a urinal for emergencies. Seeing it, she almost wished she'd gotten those lessons about peeing upright.

Almost. She'd hold it.

"What do you and Nora have planned for when we land?" he asked.

"Nora's working on booking us transport for the last leg."

"You've handled everything. Excellent."

So much for her worry that he might balk or pull some macho shit when she announced that she'd made arrangements for travel. He stretched out on a couch that only supported half his body, leaving his legs bent, and feet flat on the floor. He closed his eyes and went to sleep.

She tried to do the same but tossed and turned until he came over to her side, plucked her into the air, then lay down in her spot with her atop him.

Why protest when her eyes immediately shuttered, and her nerves calmed. She'd never been good at sleeping in places that weren't her bed. It was part of the reason she didn't travel.

Funny how snuggling Andrei relaxed her.

Even nicer was waking up with his hands on her ass, his lips in her hair. Not doing anything overt but an intimate pose, nonetheless. She wiggled in his grip. His fingers flexed before letting go.

She made a sound of protest.

"Did you have a good nap, Honeybear?" he rumbled, bringing a hand back to stroke her hair down her back.

"The best," she said, remaining splayed on his chest—wide enough to handle her. "You make a good mattress."

"Perhaps it is time we discuss me being more than a mattress for you."

"I'd rather not." Talking might ruin it.

"We fit well together."

They did. But admitting it… She wasn't ready for that. She rubbed her face into him and grunted. "No, we don't."

He laughed. "I can tell when you lie."

"Says you."

"I can. My perfect Honeybear," he murmured, nuzzling her. For a big and brash guy, he had his tender moments.

"You are slick. I can see why they say to never trust a bear."

"You can trust me."

Could she? She'd been disappointed by those who loved her in the past. An unknown father because her mom had a few too many one night in a bar. A mother who never planned to have a kid and had wandering feet.

She pushed against Andrei to sit, only to find herself straddling him. The vee between her thighs rested on the hardest part of him. She couldn't help grinding her pelvis a little.

Mmm.

She couldn't have said if that hum had come from her or him. Maybe both.

"You're going to kill me," Andrei groaned.

"Wouldn't want that." She got off him before she really *got off*. "Is that better?"

"No," he pouted, his lower lip jutting.

"I'm sure you'll get over it. There's a urinal over there if you need somewhere to put it."

That made him laugh. "I think I'd rather be blue balled."

Oddly enough, she wasn't too sure how much longer she'd last. The throb between her legs didn't understand why she stood too far away to do anything about it. "We should be getting close to the next airport."

"How much longer?"

She glanced at her watch. "The pilot said it would depend on the winds. So, could be an hour to maybe twenty minutes."

"I wouldn't need that long."

"That isn't something you should put in your personal ad."

He gaped at her and then chuckled. "Honeybear, if a man can't make you come fast when he tries, then he doesn't know what he's doing. I could make you come twice, have you dressed, and buckled in for landing in those twenty minutes."

Heat filled her. It was wrong to want it. "The pilots—"

"Are flying the plane."

She was so tempted to say, "*yes.*" But, suddenly, a speaker crackled.

"Attention, passengers. Please be seated and buckle up. We're starting our descent."

"I fucking swear something is working against me," Andrei grumbled.

He did have a point about the time never being right. Which might be why she stepped close enough to cup his face and lean in for a kiss.

As the pitch of the engines changed, he sighed into her mouth. "Better sit down, Honeybear."

The disappointment was real but mitigated by the fact that he insisted she take the spot beside his, then buckled her in and laced his fingers with hers.

Their cargo flight landed in a major South American city that wasn't their final destination. Nora had arranged for them to get a ride on a local bus. A nine-hour trip via a circuitous route, to which Andrei exclaimed, "Like fuck am I getting in one of those deathtraps. There's got to be another way. Let me see if I can rent a car. I'd rather be the one driving."

While he went looking, Hollie found a better solution. She dragged him from the rental car lineup, and it wasn't until they exited the terminal that she told him the good news.

"I've arranged a tour ride for us, by helicopter! Which is kind of cool. Always wanted to fly in one."

"They're noisy," was his observation.

"But we'll be there in just over an hour."

"I'd rather drive."

"Not me. I say quicker is better. You coming with me, or going on alone?"

"Fuck me, you drive a hard bargain, Honeybear. There'd better be air conditioning where we're going," he grumbled. "It's too fucking hot." He'd been sweating since they landed, whereas she thrived in the heat.

"Poor, Papa Bear. When we get to our destination, we'll find you a fan or something to blow on you."

"I know exactly what you can use." His gaze went to her lips, and she flushed.

But this time, rather than push him away, she uttered a coy, "Maybe. If you're good."

"I'm even better when I'm bad," was his reply as he gave her ass a light tap.

His good humor lasted until he saw the helicopter.

"That is not big enough," he declared, eyeing the bright yellow chopper.

"It's normal size for passenger-type flights," was her reply that, hopefully, hid her dubiousness. It did seem rather small.

"I'm not normal-sized," he declared.

The bear had a point. She sighed. "Then I guess we're driving. Here's to hoping your mother doesn't take the chopper in our place and get ahead of us."

"Well played, Honeybear, using my mother against me. And making the best possible argument you could."

She snorted. "You still seriously think she's going to follow us to South America?"

"Mama is coming. And it's all my fault. I told her about you."

Hollie took a moment to digest that before hesitating to ask, "Told her what exactly?"

"Enough for her to realize that we're together."

"We're not together like that. Technically." Did sleeping with him a few times in a row mean anything? They'd only shared a few kisses.

"No need to pretend with me, Honeybear. We both know this is going to get more serious and intense. And my mother will try and change that once she finds us."

Hold on. Did he actually see them getting

together? Her and chaos bear? Oh, no. Hell, no. "Just explain that we're partners. Solving a mystery like the Scooby gang."

"With me as the handsome Fred." He struck a pose.

"More like the tall, dumb Shaggy."

"Ah, you think of me as the smart and extremely popular character, who usually solves the crime."

"That would be Velma." She waved her hands. "Why are we arguing about this?"

"Because it distracts from that toy you expect me to fly in."

"Which is whose fault? We could have called your nanny. But instead, you insisted on coming out here because you're scared of your mommy," she taunted.

He leaned down and whispered, "You should be terrified, too. Because once my mother sees how I feel about you..."

"And how do you feel?" she asked, staring up at him.

"You are the one." No hesitation. No *maybe* in his statement.

"You can't be sure of that." Even as a part of her quivered in excited hope.

"I've never been more sure of anything." A vehement exclamation before he kissed her.

Her arms wound around his neck, and her lips parted. A hot sigh went from her mouth to his. He groaned as he tasted her, then ran his tongue along the contours of her mouth. The passion between them—

"Ahem. We have to leave if we're going to land before dark." their pilot interrupted. She tore her mouth from Andrei's with a snarl. He held her when she would have whirled and taken a swipe.

He sounded much too calm as he said, "Give us just a second."

"You've got thirty," snapped the pilot.

Andrei leaned down enough that his forehead touched hers. "I swear that man wants to die. His timing is shit."

"You might be right about the world conspiring to not let us finish any kisses."

He dropped a light peck on the tip of her nose. "My perfect honeybear, I promise we will have a proper uninterrupted kiss. Tonight."

"That seems too long."

"An eternity," he agreed. "I might die."

"For fuck's sake, let's go." The pilot gestured rudely as he yelled.

"You're right. He needs to die," she muttered.

"Only once we land the toy. Come on, Honeybear, let's do this before I change my mind." He gripped her hand tightly as they got into the chopper, which even she had to admit felt small when seated beside her bear.

"Isn't this cozy?" she said, not reassured at all by the flimsy seatbelt. The door clicked shut, but she didn't see a way to lock it. She really hoped that she didn't fall out. "Maybe you're right. Perhaps we should just drive." Her hand went to the buckle, ready to give up. This didn't seem like such a good idea now.

He put his hand over hers. "It will be fine."

To which the pilot turned around and said, "We need to distribute the weight a bit better."

"Meaning what?" growled Andrei.

"Meaning your fat ass needs to be in the middle, and your girlfriend needs to sit in your lap."

She wanted to protest the girlfriend part, but Andrei chose to obey the pilot and had her unclipped and in his lap within one heartbeat and the next.

The very fact that the pilot had them doing something utterly against all flight safety regulations had her wishing that she'd hired something a little bigger because Andrei was not fat. Big? Yes. But muscled all over. She'd always seen herself as average-sized, but beside him, she felt petite and dainty.

The helicopter lurched, and she tensed. To take her mind off their flight, she said, "Growing up, I always wanted a treehouse. The kind with rooms spread between some big, thick trees connected with rope bridges. What about you?"

"Castle on the ocean. Maybe in Ireland with a balcony projecting out over the cliff, catching the artic winds when they sweep."

"Sounds cold." She shuddered.

"I'd keep you warm." His arm tightened around her, and she leaned her head back against him.

"We're complete opposites," she couldn't help but remark.

"Yes."

"It would never work."

"It would." Again, calm assertion.

Could it?

When the chopper wobbled, her grip tightened enough that he murmured, "Don't be scared."

"I'm not."

"Then mind letting me have some circulation?"

She'd been sitting on his lap facing forward, fingers clutching his thighs like an oh-shit bar.

"Sorry." She put her hands on her lap.

"If anyone should be worried, it's me. Cat's land on their feet."

"So, what do bears land on?"

"Their heads." The chopper dipped, and tension coiled in him. He was nervous like she was. Which, for some reason, made her feel better.

"Explains a lot about your face."

"I thought you said I was pretty."

"Thinking I might need glasses because I should have said rugged and already banged up enough. In the future, you should land on that wide ass of yours."

He went rigid with indignation. "It is not wide."

"It is according to the pilot," she teased.

The chopper lurched, and it was her turn to swallow hard as her nerves jostled. Their ride dipped and rose, fighting a wind that was stronger at times than they were.

"It's like a roller coaster," she said with a bit of a high-pitched laugh.

"I wouldn't know. Too big to ride in them."

"It's a lot of up and down and sliding as you do loop the loops." She squirmed on him and bounced.

"All the flirting in the world won't take my mind off that fact that our flying coffin is struggling."

She winced. "Please don't call it a coffin. And I wasn't flirting."

"Says the woman grinding her ass against my cock," he whispered against her ear.

"I wasn't..." She stopped talking before he heard the lie. She was rubbing more than she should against him. The cheap thrills a teasing reminder of what she wanted from the bear.

"It's okay to admit you're attracted to me," he stated smugly.

"You're not hard on the eyes."

"Your effusive praise is embarrassing me. Stop," he said dryly.

"Smartass."

"More compliments? My bear brain might explode."

"Would you even feel it?" She couldn't help but laugh.

"Brat," he growled, digging his fingers under her arms and finding her ticklish spots. She squirmed and giggled until their pilot yelled, "Are you fucking mental?"

Apparently, because for a second, they both forgot that they were in a tiny helicopter struggling to stay out of the trees.

She stilled and glanced out the window. "Well, one good thing, I doubt anyone followed us." They were the only bird in the sky. The flight would last just under an hour.

With their flight smoother, Hollie lost her trepidation and leaned from Andrei's lap to peek outside. Everything looked so tiny. Green balls with veins of brown peeking, a lush carpet of forest below them. To their east, a mountain range smothered in more foliage.

"Check it out. It's so green," she exclaimed.

"I'm fine." Andrei remained perfectly still in the middle, staring at the back of the pilot's head. He'd not moved since their driver had chastised them.

"And people say I'm a pussy." She winked over her shoulder, and he lifted a hand to cup her face, rubbing his thumb across her lower lip.

"I can't wait to kiss you," he admitted.

"Better wait, or our pilot will give us shit again."

"I'm willing to chance it."

Her lips tilted, but a nagging thought had her saying, "Are you sure it's a good idea for us to get involved?"

"I think it's an excellent idea. We are going to have a lot of fun and adventures together."

"You're talking as if we'll keep seeing each other once this key thing is done."

"Because we will. For a long time, I predict. So long as my mother doesn't murder you."

"Is she really that crazy?"

"Crazier. But don't worry. I'll keep you safe." He

rubbed his cheek against the top of her head as she snuggled against him.

"And how will you do that from Russia?" Because he'd have to go back eventually.

"I have business interests in the USA, meaning I can visit for months at a time. And you can come see me."

"I can't just take off. I work."

"So, you work when you come to see me. I can get you contracts."

She digested that before saying, "You'd be okay with me still working as a plumber?"

"I'd rather see that than have you bumming around at home, drinking all my good vodka."

"I don't like vodka."

That had him shaking his head. "Impossible. Everyone loves good vodka. You'll see."

"Will I? You keep saying your mother won't want us to be together."

"I'll handle Mama."

Apparently, this was a time of confession, because she found herself saying, "It's not just your mother that might go a little cuckoo if we date. My family might cause a stink, too."

"Bah. I've met your aunts. I know how to handle pussycats." He angled her face for a kiss. Their lips touched, and it was instant attraction. Insane passion.

Panting breaths. Hot, pulsing heat. Her world being rocked.

Quite literally. But not because they were out of control.

"Something's wrong," she huffed.

"It feels right to me." He tugged her bottom lip, but she pulled away, her gaze suddenly drawn by the dark blur that streaked past the window. Whir, splatter.

She saw some of the remains go spinning past. Then more dark streaks, and thumps as if something had hit the carapace of the chopper.

"What the fuck?" Andrei exclaimed.

Their pilot was the one to reply. "Something must have disturbed a nest of bats. Hold on."

Bats? Hollie could see through the cockpit window and gaped as a veritable cloud of bodies suddenly enveloped them. Thock. Tock. Whack. Bump.

The winged rodents hit the body of the chopper and tangled in the rotors. The more ominous noise was the choking of the motors.

Then the silence as they died.

CHAPTER ELEVEN

When the engine on the helicopter died, that wasn't the time to say, "*I told you so.*" Andrei had known better than to get on the tiny deathtrap, and now that he'd been proven right, it was time to plan how they'd survive the crash.

He braced himself as Hollie asked, "Think there are parachutes on board?"

"Even if there are, we're not high enough to deploy them," he remarked. "We need to prepare for impact."

"Prepare how? By pulling an airbag out of our asses?" Her sarcasm didn't completely hide her fear.

"I won't let you die." A bold statement that he quickly followed up with, "Why are you so worried? You're a cat."

"We don't always land on our feet," she muttered.

"I think," he said, trying to ignore the whistling as they lost altitude, "that you should promise me a kiss if we walk away from this."

"I'll give you more than that if we do."

"Tuck your face into me," was the last thing he said before they hit the jungle treetops.

Crackle. Crunch.

They jostled and jumped, but Andrei kept hold of Hollie throughout. Even when the wreck's descent abruptly halted, dangling them at an angle, he kept his grip. Everything not strapped down went flying, including their bag. It dropped through the gap into the front of the chopper and landed on the curve of the windshield. Through it, he had a great view of how far they'd fall.

"You alive?" yelled the pilot.

"Yeah. But we need to get out before this thing starts moving again." Their precarious position kept him from making any abrupt motions.

"Anyone else smell smoke?" asked Hollie.

"I smell it." Never a good thing.

Hollie tapped the hands holding her. "Let me see if I can open the door. She balanced with her feet braced on the edge of the frame. While she crouched to check on it, Andrei looked for handholds before shifting his feet.

"Any idea how far we are from the nearest town?" he asked their pilot, who stood on his windshield and held on to his seat to face them.

"We were about ten minutes from landing. Meaning, still an hour or more walk in this terrain," the human complained.

"An hour? That's nothing," Hollie scoffed. She

TAMING A BEAR   123

heaved at the mechanism for the door. It didn't budge.
"It's stuck. Can you open it?" she asked Andrei.

"Does a bear shit in the woods?"

"Only the ones who aren't housebroken," was her
saucy reply.

He laughed. "You can tame me anytime,
Honeybear."

"Maybe I will, Papa Bear."

Their pilot scowled at them. "Not the time to play
kissy face. We need to get out of the bird."

"You are really making me hungry," Andrei grumbled as he heaved at the lever on the door.

Hollie giggled. "Probably too stringy."

"Might need tenderizing first," he agreed, heaving
again. Only the door wouldn't budge.

"I think it's stuck," the pilot stated as if that weren't
obvious.

"We'll need to find another way out," Hollie stated,
running her fingers over the frame. The window on the
door was a single piece intersected by a cage of metal.
The same on the side without the door. Meanwhile,
the smoke thickened.

"We'll have to get out via the cockpit." Andrei
pointed, they all looked down, and before he could say
move, the pilot shifted his stance and stomped on the
windshield. It creaked.

"You idiot, stop that." Andrei felt the chopper
tremble as the impact jolted its fragile perch.

"We need to get out of here before we burn
alive." The pilot was in a full-blown panic as he

slammed his foot down again. The window spiderwebbed.

"Hold on tight," Andrei told Hollie.

Before the pilot could wind up for a third kick, the helicopter shifted with a groan of metal.

Screee.

The human lost his balance and hit the splintered glass hard on his butt. It didn't hold.

The pieces tumbled, taking the pilot with them. His scream lasted until he landed.

"It's a long way down," Hollie noted.

"At least, he won't be interrupting us anymore."

She glanced at him. Arched a brow.

"Too soon?"

"The man *did* just die."

"Because he forgot basic gravity. Be careful."

"You be careful. I don't need you taking me out if you slip."

"Would you prefer I go first, then?"

"Are you implying I'm going to fall?"

"Have you climbed many trees?"

"Just try and keep up, Papa Bear." She dropped down, using the pilot's seat to break her descent before gripping the edge of the window frame and slipping out.

Smoke filled the cabin.

"If I make it to the ground first, I should get a prize," he stated as he quickly followed.

"Beat me there, and I'll give you a kiss."

"And if you beat me?" he stated, dangling by his

fingertips from the windshield frame, hearing the entire helicopter groan. The branch she'd used might be a little too skinny for him. His toes reached for a thicker one.

"If I win...you get to sleep, and *only* sleep, with me so I can use you as a pillow tonight."

"Well that's just plain cruel," he complained.

"Then don't lose," she trilled. Hollie, already a branch below him, had kicked off her sandals and hiked up her summer dress, flashing her bare legs as she climbed. He quickly began to follow, using his brute strength to lower himself to another limb. It held his weight.

The branches overhead rustled, bending at the intruder in their midst. He glanced at the chopper, preciously hanging just over him and Hollie.

"We need to get out of this tree," he stated.

The chopper creaked and shifted, showering pieces of branches and leaves.

"Oh, shit," she muttered, hugging a trunk and moving around it towards a spot where she could make a run at the next tree.

"Faster!" he yelled, jumping down a few branches to reach her spot. She'd hesitated, looking back for him.

He grabbed her hand to run across the fat forking limb. The other tree was so close yet so far as a mighty crack sounded overhead.

They had no more time. Andrei wound an arm around Hollie's waist. His other hand grabbed a vine and twisted it around his wrist. Having lost his loafers, his toes dug in as he ran the few feet left on the branch before jumping.

And yes, he uttered a Tarzan yell. They hit the next tree just in time. With a groan and a shudder, the helicopter started to plummet, dragging branches with it, and shoving at a few trees, knocking one completely over.

When a tree fell in a forest, the whole world shook, hard enough Andrei slipped off the branch he balanced on and swung away. He had to wait for the backswing before his toes scraped across bark. He gripped it and arced his body until he had his balance.

"Holy shit," Hollie breathed. "I can't believe that vine held us."

"Now that was some Tarzan type stuff right there," he exclaimed with a broad grin as he set her down beside him on the thick branch.

She held on to him for a second before murmuring, "I'm starting to see how you lose your luggage and ruin your clothes."

"Losing it because my transportation crashed in the jungle is new. Most of the time, it's because my mother sets fire to my suitcases."

"I don't know if you're fucking with me or serious."

He smiled. "If I'm fucking you, it will be serious. Intense. And pleasurable."

She flushed, and not because of the heat. "Once again foiled by circumstance, though."

"Hardly. You heard our pilot. We are probably

only an hour from town. You'll be writhing on sheets by tonight."

He didn't miss the dilation of her eyes or the hitch in her breath. He couldn't resist leaning close, keeping her safe at the thickest vee of the branch where it met the tree.

"Need I remind you, Papa Bear? You haven't won the bet yet." She ducked and slid out from the cage of his arms. "See you at the bottom," she crooned as she popped down a branch.

"Oh yes, you will." Because he was winning the kiss she'd promised.

Only she proved agile, moving rapidly, her smaller size giving her more branches to work with. When she hit the ground, she kept moving, away from the wreck, which was smart.

When she stopped, it was sudden, and she flung her arms around his neck. "I won."

"The race to the bottom. But what about the more than a kiss you promised if we didn't die?"

"Does someone need a consolation prize?" she asked, her tone quite coy.

"I just need you."

She stood on tiptoe, and because she was still too short, he lifted her so she could slant her mouth over his. Hot. Steamy. Soft. Parting.

He groaned at the touch of her tongue. The taste of her. He had her back against a tree without even thinking twice about it.

His hand slid up the hem of her dress, skimming

her ribs to cup the cotton of her bra. His thumb brushed over the peak, and he felt her nipple pucker behind the fabric.

She moaned and arched into him, thrusting her hips. Parting her thighs around his leg and pressing.

Her need seemed frantic, and he knew why. The adrenaline of surviving. The thrill of having cheated death. Now, she wanted to celebrate by feeling even more alive.

He dropped to his knees before her and nudged up the hem of her skirt.

"We shouldn't," was her breathy suggestion, even as her fingers twined in his hair.

"Give me a good reason why."

"Birth control."

"Can't get you pregnant with my mouth or fingers," he said, blowing hotly on her. He nuzzled at her underpants, and she moaned. The scent of her. The wetness. The arousal.

She couldn't hide it from him. She writhed with need. Desire had her murmuring, "What are you waiting for?"

Permission received, he tugged down those panties with his teeth, far enough that they fell and weren't in his way. He parted her thighs, lifting a leg so it rested on his shoulder, exposing her to him.

He took full advantage, lapping at her honeyed sex. Parting her nether lips to feel the shivering heat of her. Finding her clit and playing it, strumming that swollen nub until she panted his name and tugged on his hair.

He thrust fingers into her as he licked and tugged. Pumped harder and felt her tighten around him, her whole body tensing, her mouth opening. Wider. Her breath halted. Her entire being coiled.

Then, she came.

She came so fucking hard on his fingers. Against his mouth. She climaxed, screaming his name.

And he'd never felt so fucking aroused in his life.

Until something landed on his head.

CHAPTER TWELVE

"It's not funny," he grumbled for the umpteenth time, his cheeks still a ruddy color.

"I think it's adorable that a big, strong guy like you is scared of spiders."

"Not normal-sized ones. That thing was the size of my fist. And hairy!" he exclaimed. He cast a suspicious eye on the tree branches overhead. "It was hideous."

"And harmless to our kind, I'll bet. It was probably more scared of you."

"Doubtful." Said with an adorable scowl.

She wondered how much of that had to do with frustration. While she'd had an epic orgasm, the poor guy had gotten the fright of his life when that enormous spider landed on his head and decided to explore.

The shrieks that came out of her bear...

If only she'd been taping it. Instead, she'd scrounged for her underwear, which had some kind of bugs swarming over the crotch when she lifted it. On second thought, she began unbuttoning her dress.

"I don't think sex is a good idea out here with those things." Again, he squinted at the canopy of green overhead.

"I'd say the mood for that has passed. I can't walk for an hour with no underwear or shoes. Let's go four-legged."

"We'll be naked when we get to town," he warned.

"Don't tell me that's never happened to you before."

He rolled his broad shoulders. "All the time. It's how I know that people sometimes get a little upset when you appear with dangling bits."

She put a hand on her hip. "You think someone will have a problem with this?" She glanced down at her body quickly before peeking at him to see him staring.

It was cruel. But she felt powerful after her orgasm. In charge.

"You can't let anyone see you," he moaned. "Because then I'd have to kill them, and that might be difficult to explain."

Jealousy? Over her? She should have been above it. Yet, it thrilled her.

"Ready, Papa Bear?" She stepped close and tilted her head to look at him. He practically smoldered with need. But he wasn't an animal.

Not about his arousal. He murmured, "The moment we find a bed, Honeybear."

He didn't finish that thought. Didn't have to.

She shifted and waited only a second to make sure that he followed before bolting. There was something exhilarating about having him chase her. He was huge, compared to her. In a fight, he'd dominate through sheer size alone. And yet, this big man had dropped to his knees to pleasure her.

She could change right now and ask, and she'd wager that he'd do it again.

The temptation to do it slowed her steps, and he charged past her, a big, lumbering, hairy ass and a snuffling snort that had her sprinting to pull ahead again.

Only as the smell of civilization hit them, did they slow and become more careful, following a thin thread of smoke to a house in the woods. It was set in a space cleared of trees, with a clothesline strung and bowing in the sunshine.

While he kept watch, she headed for the drying clothes, hiding behind a hanging sheet. She snatched what was easiest and closest. The oversized button-down shirt hit her only an inch above the knee when donned, voluminous around her enough that she grabbed a hanging stocking and used it as a belt. She forewent underwear.

While the shirt could have wrapped around her a few times, a t-shirt of cotton that seemed just as wide, barely fit her bear. As for the pants? She bit her lip so as not to laugh, given that they were skintight and short on him.

"Maybe I should fashion a loincloth instead."

She almost said, "*do it.*" He would look fabulous with no shirt and only a skimpy covering for below his waist. "We need to move before someone notices we've taken their stuff."

"Once I get my hands on a phone with online shopping, remind me to have something sent to this house," he stated as they followed the ruts of trail out to a road.

"With what? You lost your credit card in the crash."

"Given this might have happened to me before, I memorized the login for a few online shopping portals already preset with my card number."

"Handy. Do you have an online service that provides jungle rescue?"

"We'll be fine."

She snorted. "Your optimism is astounding. But I'd rather not count on luck. I'll borrow a phone in the next village and call the Pride for assistance."

"I wouldn't recommend that. By now, my mother will have been in contact with your lion king. He will be obliged to tell her our location."

"Arik wouldn't if we asked him not to."

"My mother will get the information out of him. It's her superpower. She just stares and stares until you blurt all your secrets."

She snorted. "Less superpower and more like a guilty conscience. You really are a mama's boy."

"Is that a problem?"

"I don't know. Is it? You're the one who insisted we fly to South America to escape."

"Or I saw an excuse to go on a tropical vacation with my honeybear."

"A vacation implies a room with plumbing, sheets, and cocktails."

"I promise, tonight we will sleep in a bed."

"A vacation also means taking selfies and posting them online with stupid hashtags."

"If you want to post images, then we can. At least then, they'll have something recent to use when looking for your body."

She slugged him. "Stop saying that your mom is going to kill me. Especially since you're apparently going to do nothing to stop it!" Hollie had had enough of his macabre prediction.

"I am doing something. I'm keeping the two of you apart."

"Why are you so convinced your mother is going to hate me on sight? Is it because I'm a lion?"

"Partly. But mostly because, one day, you'll be my wife."

"W-w-what?" was what she finally stuttered.

But did he explain what he meant? Nope. He strolled along, whistling, a barefoot vagabond with a smile tugging at the corners of his lips.

And she might have fallen in love in that second.

They entered the village, toes dusty, and poor Andrei dripping in sweat. Big Russian bear used to a colder climate didn't fare so well in the humid jungle

TAMING A BEAR   135

heat. She absolutely loved the warmth. Whether it be somewhere tropical or cuddled against someone.

The village, a place with what looked like maybe two dozen or so buildings, bustled more than she would have expected. People of all sizes wandered, some carrying baskets and bags. Children chased each other and balls. Animals wandered freely; chickens, a pig, a few goats. Scooters hummed past along with carts drawn by mules and other beasts of burden.

It was only as the entire village appeared to stop and everybody suddenly stared at them that she wondered how often strangers came to visit. And on foot no less. Not many, she'd wager. Or was the open hostile appraisal because they recognize the clothes?

The longer it went on, the more it unnerved.

Andrei broke the impasse. "Hello. I'm Andrei Medvedev. Looking for my nanny, Mila Miskouri. Anyone know where I can find her?"

"Medvedev." The name was mumbled, and the whispering in the crowd increased, but not in English, so she couldn't figure out what was being said. The villagers spread out to form a circle around them, faces angry.

Hollie edged close to Andrei. "What's happening?"

"I'm not sure, but gauging by their expressions, they're pissed."

"Do they know we stole the clothes?" She glanced down. Perhaps the faded blue cotton shirt was familiar. "We didn't hurt anyone. I swear. Although, our helicopter pilot is dead because of the crash. But we had nothing to do with it!" She raised her hands to show innocence.

"I don't think that helped," he muttered as the crowd eased in closer. Andrei put an arm around her and held out his free hand. "Don't come any closer."

"You are being arrested," spat one of the older, thicket men, his hair sprinkled with gray.

"For what? I didn't kill our pilot. And if it's about the clothes we borrowed, I was already planning to pay for them generously as soon as I get to a phone."

"You are a Medvedev. You know a Lada?" asked the guy leading the mob.

"Yeah I know her. She's my sister," he muttered with a pained expression. "Have you seen her?"

"We did. And as a result of your sister's actions, you are under arrest. Take him." The old man pointed, and the villagers approached, machetes in hand, cudgels at the ready.

Quickly, Hollie assessed her options. Fight? There were too many humans present. She couldn't shift to give herself an advantage. Neither could Andrei. They could try and fight, but without the battle skill of their beasts, they'd be overwhelmed. Especially since they probably shouldn't kill anyone. It would draw too much attention.

"I'll come with you, but you will not lay a hand on my woman."

His woman? She glanced at him, his stony expression intent on the old man who ventured the closest.

"She is being taken to jail too as your accomplice." The crowd grew braver and surged to within striking distance.

Andrei stiffened and muttered, "Stay behind me. I'll handle this."

"As if I'm going to let you fight alone. You take the dozen on the left, I've got the right. Whoever finishes first gets the stragglers."

"I won't let anyone hurt you," was his solemn promise as the villagers neared, a mob currently brave only because they had no idea what they faced.

Would Hollie die to keep her secret? She doubted that Andrei would.

He didn't act until Hollie squeaked because someone had tossed a rock that hit her.

At her pained cry, Andrei flexed, gaining in size, even as he held back the fur. His fingers were tipped in claws, and she'd bet if he opened his mouth, he'd have some sharp teeth.

It took only seconds, and then he whirled. With a roar, he charged into the crowd.

That started the screaming. People not interested in a fight, fled, scattering chickens, and dogs, scooping up children. Those brave enough to face an enraged man rushed for Andrei, who knocked them around, probably breaking a few bones. But given they were trying to cave in his head, understandable.

Someone even ran at Hollie, a wild-eyed woman with a cleaver. Hollie caught the arm as it started its descent, holding the blade away from her face, ignoring the open-mouthed yodeling. She would have to hurt this lady, who smelled of baby spit-up and flour.

A sharp whistle cut through the air, and the person she strained against stiffened before going loose-limbed. Another whistle had the crowd disengaging. All around, combatants picked themselves up off the ground, groaning and holding injured parts.

No one was dead or severely wounded. More than a few did cast Andrei a side-eye, though. He bared his teeth, his normal teeth, at them, making a few flinch, and others cross themselves.

The leader of the mob went to confront the old woman who'd entered the village square with its stone-rimmed well. Hollie sat on its edge and dipped into the water bucket for a drink. Watching so that she might understand what had happened.

The old lady shooed the gesticulating and jabbering man. The mob leader scowled and stomped off, leaving behind Mila Miskouri, who leaned heavily on a cane, wore a thick sweater, and sported a bruise on her face.

"Nanny." Andrei, no longer the fearsome half-beast but the smiling, happy guy she'd gotten to know, took a step towards the woman.

Miskouri eyed him for a moment. Lips pursed. "Another trouble-causing Medvedev."

"Wasn't my fault. They attacked first," he muttered with a sulking lower lip.

"Only because of what your sister did to me."

His face tightened. "She hurt you?" At her nod,

Andrei hung his head, and Hollie could feel the shame pouring off him. "I'm sorry."

Mila Miskouri uttered a heavy sigh before saying, "I know you are. And you're not to blame for her actions. Let's go somewhere private where we can talk." The village lady with her cleaver gestured wildly, but Miskouri said only a single word, and the woman quieted.

They followed her slow-moving figure, leaning hard on her cane, only until they reached the jungle's edge. Then, Miskouri straightened, and the cane became more something to swing than to rely on. Andrei's nanny tossed a look over her shoulder.

"Before you ask, yes, I was faking. I need to slow down my healing, or the villagers will notice there's something different about me." Because Miskouri with her curly hair mostly gray and slightly wrinkled dark features was a shifter. A type of bear but not a flavor she'd experienced before.

"What are you?" Hollie asked. She'd rather be blunt than say something ignorant later on.

"Andean. Some call us the spectacled bears. We're rare. So rare that I only know of one other like me."

"Does that mean you'll go extinct?" Hollie asked. A few of the shifter lines had over the centuries. Eagles being the most recent. They'd also lost the dolphins. Either that or they simply didn't come ashore anymore.

Miskouri pointed her cane as she replied, "We might. Or somewhere, someday, a recessive gene will activate." Because only rarely did the mixing of species result in hybrids. Most times, the child bonded more tightly with one animal form than the other. The stronger, more dominant gene like eye color or freckles. But that didn't mean the other animal disappeared completely.

"We have an aunt who, despite having two lion parents, was born with orange stripes. It caused quite a row until a DNA test showed that she actually was their cub."

"We had genetic tests run on Lada a few times because we could never figure out how our family got stuck with her," Andrei said lightly, but Hollie heard the undercurrent.

"Is your sister really that awful?"

He waved a hand at his nanny. "Why don't you ask her?"

"I'm afraid she's what you might call a bad seed. Almost every family has one. A person without the same morals as the rest. Who thinks only of themselves and doesn't care about the harm they cause."

"You thought she'd changed," Hollie said softly.

"Yes, and I fell for the act. Lada came here pretending that she wanted to visit with me because she was feeling nostalgic. I should have known better. A vicious brat as a child, even more so as an adult," was Miskouri's vehement reply.

"Lada beat you," Andrei stated, and Hollie could see the tension thrumming within him.

"Not her, but her companions. She stood by and watched as they attacked me. she didn't stop it either."

"What companions?" Andrei asked.

Miskouri's lips flattened. "Your sister is working with humans."

Which led to the next most important question. "Do they know about us?" As a child, Hollie's first lesson on being a shifter was to never reveal what you are.

"I don't know. They didn't act as if they did. And Lada didn't do anything inhuman. So, neither did I. I could have stopped them otherwise." Miskouri raised a hand to her still-bruised cheek. They must have hit her hard for it to still be so dark.

"What did Lada and her companions want from you?" Andrei asked.

"A book."

He halted in his tracks. "The one you used to read to us when we were children?"

"Yes. Your sister stole it."

CHAPTER THIRTEEN

The knowledge that Andrei had just missed his sister burned. Mostly because seeing his nanny's face bruised, a woman he and his sister had once hugged, and on his part at least, loved, he wondered if Lada was truly that depraved. She used to at least have some boundaries. Did she really have no morals anymore?

"Where did she go?" he asked. Because if Nanny was still bruised, then it couldn't have happened long ago.

"I imagine she went back to the city. She arrived in some large SUV this morning with her companions armed to the teeth. Left an hour later the same way."

"Meaning, she's only a few hours ahead of us." The late-afternoon sun made that more than the couple he seemed to think. "Do you know of a vehicle we can buy or borrow?"

"What happened to yours? Don't tell me you walked." Nanny eyed their feet.

"Only after our helicopter crashed." He quickly explained what had happened, and Nanny tsked.

"Mani knew better than to shortcut over those caves." She turned off onto a dirt path that showed signs of recent use, the shrubbery lining it cracked and torn as if something large had pushed its way through.

The line of bushes and trees halted at the edge of a clearing. Nanny didn't live in a treehouse or a wattle hut made of mud and grass. She'd had a real home built, with a stucco exterior, a shingle roof holding a few solar panels, and a screened-in front porch. Inside, she'd adopted a beachy retreat style that involved lots of wicker and aquatic décor—such as seashells and a few porcelain sea creatures scattered on the surfaces. The kitchen opened to a seating area with a couch, chairs, and a low-slung table.

Andrei saw two other doors, one through which he could see tile. A bathroom. He hoped with a shower because there was no air conditioning. Just a lazy fan spinning slowly in the peaked roof.

"Lemonade? Cookies?" asked Nanny.

"Yes, please." He almost started drooling.

Then he tasted the lemonade, which was all tart lemon and no sugary aid. The cookies appeared made of seed and tasted healthy, which was a flavor. Kind of dry with no sweet or salty. Just lots of chewing.

Hollie nibbled without making a face and smiled at

his nanny. "Thank you for rescuing us. We had no idea what we'd be getting into coming out here."

He could have snorted. He knew what happened when he went places. Chaos. Which, on second thought, he might not want to point out. Hollie had made it clear that she wasn't into drama.

Nanny drank the lemonade without puckering her cheeks. "I grew up in a village like this one. It got mowed down about two decades ago. But when I retired, I couldn't stop thinking of it."

"It's nice," Hollie said.

"If you ignore the fact that the spiders are huge," Andrei muttered.

Nanny shot him a sharp look. "Excuse me. Manners. I'm having a conversation with the young lady."

"Sorry." He ducked his head.

"Hmph." His nanny turned back to Hollie. "We were never actually introduced. I'm Mila Miskouri, but you may call me Nanny."

"I'm Hollie."

"Such a lovely name." Nanny patted Hollie's hand. "Now, tell me how you came to be here with little Andrei. Are you helping him locate his sister?"

Little? Did his nanny need glasses?

"We didn't even know she was in South America. We actually came because of an old key that recently resurfaced. Andrei thought he recognized a symbol on it." She glossed over the issues attached to the heirloom.

"Lada asked about a key, but I didn't know what she was talking about at first. And then she started questioning me about the princess story."

"What princess story?" Hollie asked.

His nanny glanced at him. "Do you remember it?"

He shook his head.

"It's a simple one, a variation of one told around the world, about a prince who is a monster, and a princess who loves him. However, they can't be together until he finds a spell that turns him into a man."

"What does the story have to do with a key?" Hollie asked.

"In the book, the chest he finds needs a key. A special one etched with magical symbols."

"Because the lock can't be picked. Nor can the chest be broken open," was Andrei's contribution.

Nanny nodded. "You do remember parts of it."

"I remember not liking the fact that it was a love story." He grimaced. "Why would anyone want to be anything but the beast?"

"Not everyone embraces who they are. Your sister, for example. She never liked being a bear."

"She didn't like a lot of things," Andrei remarked. She hated everything, everyone. Lada complained, and he tuned her out. But maybe he shouldn't have. He should have listened when she said that she wasn't comfortable in her body. "Does she think the key leads to an actual magical box with a remedy to stop her from being a bear?"

His nanny rolled her shoulders. "She didn't say. But she wants that key."

"Too bad, so sad. She can't have it," Hollie stated.

"You have it?" Nanny asked.

"More or less," was Hollie's vague reply. "I left it in a safe place since I was worried about it getting stolen or lost on the trip."

So much for his belief that she'd swallowed it. Not the most comfortable smuggling solution, but it worked. He just wouldn't discuss the discomfort of removal.

"You've seen it, though." His nanny leaned forward. "Can you describe it?"

"I could try," Hollie said hesitantly. "It was about this big." Her hands started out far apart, then closer, then smudging a little wide. "I think."

This would be painful, so Andrei interrupted. "I can do better than that. I need a pencil and a sheet of paper."

"What's the magic word?" Nanny eyed him.

"Please."

In short order, he'd sketched the key, and then a larger version of the symbol he recalled.

His nanny snared it and brought it close. She said nothing for a long moment before saying, "I can see why you came looking for the book."

"It's the same symbol as in that story," Andrei stated.

"So it appears."

"Well, now we know why people are after the key. It opens some kind of treasure box."

"Does it?" Nanny cast doubt. "Until your sister showed up, and now you, it was just a story. I'd never heard of the key actually existing. And do we really believe there's a magical box somewhere with a way to subdue the beast within?"

"Is it so farfetched given there are drugs to suppress almost anything? And in the story, wasn't this a permanent solution and not something that wears off over time?" he reminded.

Hollie had risen from the chair to pace while hugging her body. "Lada obviously believes it exists. But her actions seem extreme given all she's looking for is a spell to make her human."

"Is it her, though, that wants it?" Nanny asked. "I am not sure she is acting entirely of her own volition."

"You think the humans are controlling her?" Andrei wanted to latch on to that tiny thread of hope that his sister wasn't pure evil.

"I think there is much we don't know about this situation other than that some people are chasing after a fable in a children's book."

"And using force along the way," he muttered.

Hollie was the one to ask, "Why take the book? How does that help her? Does it have a map of some sort?"

"I don't think so." Andrei wracked his brain for a recollection of the illustrations.

Nanny knew it better than him. "No map.

However, there are clues sprinkled throughout his quest."

"Something about a beach, then a volcano." Andrei frowned as he tried to remember.

"You forget the cave that is trapped and the monster before the box," Nanny added.

"Is there a mention of where this story takes place?" Hollie tapped her lower lip. "Even without the key, Lada might be going for the treasure."

"If we knew where she was going, we might be able to head her off." Andrei sprang to his feet.

Nanny dashed any hope for an easy fix. "I always assumed an imaginary land as it spoke of the burning cold desert, the refracting diamond plane, the cliffs on the edge of the world."

Hollie grimaced. "A set of coordinates would have been more useful."

"We just need to decipher the riddle," was Andrei's more optimistic take.

"If it were that easy, it would have been found by now," was Hollie's skeptical observation.

"If you ask me, it should stay hidden." He'd been keen on finding what the key unlocked until he found out the truth. Render a magnificent shifter into a mere human?

Never. The very idea horrified.

Which was why Lada and her human partners couldn't get their hands on it. While not one to give in to conspiracy theories, he couldn't see any good coming of humans knowing how to eradicate his kind. It would mean the end of everything.

"Since we don't know where to go, we should try to find Lada's trail. You said she left this morning. More than likely to get back to the city and fly out to her next destination."

"Not according to my sources. Apparently, they had a flat, which took some time to repair. While they were fixing it, word got out about what they did. They're currently on foot after their SUV suffered an accident with a tree."

"Meaning, we could catch them."

"Or get ahead of them," his nanny declared. "Last word had them heading north for the train tracks. There's a run going through those mountains tomorrow morning."

"Can we get to the train before them?" Andrei asked.

"Depends on if you're afraid of heights."

"Give me a cape, and I'll jump off anything," he declared, thumping his chest.

Hollie, on the other hand, played it cautious. "I assume whatever you're suggesting won't kill us?"

"Accidents are rare. And don't cats land on their feet?" Nanny eyed Hollie, who shook her head.

"What is it with bears assuming that?" she muttered.

"When do we leave?" he asked.

"Midnight. You'll be able to catch a ride without any of their spotters seeing you."

Given it wasn't even five o'clock, they had time to bathe, clothe themselves with Nanny's aid, eat—and make it almost edible once he added a shaker full of salt—and think about taking a nap.

What he didn't get? Alone time with Holly. The curse that kept him from kissing her properly continued with Nanny's tendency to pop in at the most inopportune moments.

The second his old nursemaid went outside for some air before bed, he dragged Hollie into his arms for a long kiss.

When he let her up for air, she managed a breathy, "We shouldn't. Your nanny might come in anytime."

"Or she left to give us privacy."

He waggled his brows just as his cockblocking nursemaid reentered the house. "None of that." She waved a switch and stung his hand with it. "Not under my roof while you're unmated."

"Er, what?"

"A lady doesn't give it away without commitment. Nor does a gentleman ask." Nanny lifted her chin. "Come, Hollie. You should rest before your adventure. You'll share the bedroom with me."

"But—"

There were no buts. Nanny dragged Hollie to her bed, while Andrei got to squish himself onto the uncomfortable wicker couch.

He'd just prepared to spend the worst night ever when Nanny came marching out of his room, grumbling. "She is a restless sleeper."

"I know."

"Move."

Nanny kicked him off the couch, and he got the bed. He slid in, and Hollie immediately climbed on top. "About time, I thought she'd never leave," she murmured against his chest.

And while his blue balls would probably fall off, he'd never been happier.

CHAPTER FOURTEEN

Happiness was waking on top of Andrei's chest. Pure joy would have been doing something about the erection poking at her.

However, a chirped, "Get up and get moving if you're going to catch that train," put an end to any thoughts of wakeup sex. They truly were cursed.

Nanny gave them a quick snack and then ordered them to shift.

"What?"

"You'll make better time up the mountain to the Aerie."

"We'll be naked when we arrive," Hollie pointed out.

"No, you won't." Nanny had packed a pair of satchels with clothes not stolen and more suited to their size. The straps of the bags were wound around their bodies after they'd shifted.

Nanny hugged them each and then cackled when

Andrei's wet bear nose rubbed her. "Remember, up the mountain to the vee between the peaks. Once there, it's a short flight to the bottom and the train tracks."

Sounded so simple, it made her wonder why they'd not taken this route to come here. Only to totally understand once they reached the pass through the mountainous humps. There was a shack up here, and a spool of wire that extended from where it was staked into the rock, down over the edge of the cliff. The very steep cliff.

"Please tell me there's a cute little gondola to ride in," she said as they changed into their clothes out of sight.

"I think those straps are it," he indicated, pointing out the hanging loops hung on a hook beside the contraption.

"We'll die."

"Or have a grand adventure."

"Calling death an adventure doesn't make it more appealing, you know."

He snared her close. "I won't let you fall."

"I know you won't. But still..." She leaned her head on him. "I miss plumbing."

"And I miss having a real bed," he lamented. Where they could snuggle. Naked. And uninterrupted. "Soon, Honeybear. We'll be done with all this, and we can enjoy a quiet life."

"Not too quiet, I hope." She squeezed his ass, enjoyed the surprise on his face, and then sauntered to the shack. It was run by a corpulent woman and her partner. The pair of them thick and strong. Also, hard negotiators who took almost everything Miskouri sent them off with.

Then they got their heavily accented instructions. "Hold on until the bottom."

"That's it? What about a safety harness? Maybe a *'don't worry, it's not that far.'*"

"It's far. Hold on." The gap-toothed grin did nothing to reassure.

"Just grab on to me, Honeybear. I've got this."

Much as Hollie would like to, that would add a lot of weight for him to bear. "I can do this." She was strong.

She grabbed hold of the strap, took a deep breath, and before she could let it out, the wire jerked and yanked her forward, dragging her feet off the edge with a scream.

"Hollie!" She heard the slight panic in Andrei's voice, and his muttered, "I should have gone first." Because he thought she needed rescuing.

She gritted her teeth and held on. She could do this. How long could it take to reach the bottom?

Longer than she liked. She had a chance to watch in the distance the sinuous arrival of the train, its headlights projecting through the darkness. They'd be cutting it close.

After an eternity, the ground approached, along with another shack where a short man exited, cigarette dangling from his lips. He squinted at them before shouting, "Jump."

A glance down showed the ground too far.

"Jump and run, or you won't make the train," he said in a heavy accent.

Eight feet. Seven. She leaped and hit the ground with her knees bent.

She took a staggering step, then found her hand gripped as Andrei bolted past her, snaring her in his wake.

"Run, Honeybear. Run like bees are chasing you."

Now wasn't the time to admit that she'd never disturbed a comb because she wasn't a dumbass. She lifted her knees and ran with him, aiming for the slight incline that held the tracks. Hearing the chug of the train as it neared, then a sharp whistle and the impression of something soaring overhead.

Before she could ask, Andrei answered. "Goods." Because they were using a smuggler's route.

They ran parallel to the rails as the train tore past, the wind of it dragging them along.

She saw the handles welded to the cars. The idea was simple. Grab hold and climb on.

But the train moved quickly. She reached and missed, the bar ripping out of her hand, causing her to stumble. An arm came around and swept her off her feet. Andrei had grabbed on to the bar behind her.

He held her close and whooped. "Made it, Honeybear."

"You've done this before," she stated.

"Maybe one or a dozen times. I love a slow, scenic ride. Let's find a spot to hunker."

"Shouldn't we watch for when your sister gets on?"

"That's not for a while yet. Come." He found them a bower inside a trailer with a narrow passageway through it, stacked with bags of grain. They made a malleable bed when they climbed to the top.

"How long do we have before we need to keep watch?" she asked as they stretched out.

"From what Nanny said, probably a few hours."

"Weren't you the one who said he only needed twenty minutes?" It was bold, but then again, given what kept happening...past time.

"I might have lied. I want you for more than twenty minutes or even an hour. I don't think an eternity of pleasuring you will be enough," he growled, drawing her near.

She reached out to cup his cheek in the semigloom. "Then maybe we should start."

He dipped his head to kiss her. This time, she didn't have to strain to reach since they were lying down. His lips slanting over hers, only to lose focus as she sucked on his bottom lip. He hummed, a vibration that made her quiver.

Desire filled her as their teeth clashed, and their breaths meshed hotly. Without interruption, they devoured each other. Until he decided to go exploring, dragging his lips over her jawline then down her neck, finding her sweet spots and grazing them with his teeth. A good thing she lay down because she trembled. Weak with desire. She tugged at his hand and sucked at the finger she'd inserted into her mouth.

He growled.

Mmmm. Someone liked that.

She sucked harder as he rolled half atop her, inserting a thigh between her legs and rubbing, teasing her most sensitive spot. His free hand roamed, finding her erogenous zones, stroking them, teasing her, sensitizing her skin to the point she wanted to tear off all her clothes. Actually...

She took a moment to strip, and he followed suit until they were both naked on top of the bags of grain. Skin to skin, at least. The hair on his body created a friction that had her shivering as they kissed and writhed.

She shoved him onto his back at one point, fully aware it was his turn for some fun. Rising up, her knees digging into the sack of grain, she leaned down and brushed her lips over the tip of his fat cock—thick and hard like the rest of him.

A glance at his face showed his expression smoldering. Burning with desire.

She held his length and, quirking her lips into a taunting smile, licked the tip of him. His hips jerked.

She lapped again, and his jaw clenched. She took the fat head into her mouth and sucked, and he hissed even as his hips twitched again.

She had him at her mercy, writhing at her touch, and soon, she was bobbing on his cock with him grunting, "No, slow down. I won't be able to hold— Aww." He came.

Hot and salty on her tongue. Quickly, too, so she laughed as she licked him clean.

But didn't laugh for long as he bearhandled her so that they were in a sixty-nine position with her on her back, her legs spread, and his face buried between her thighs. His semi-hard cock poked at her lips. Apparently, they weren't done.

Could he get hard that quickly again? She began to suck at him to find out, only to gasp as his tongue flicked against her clit.

She moaned. Mewled. She sucked and panted as he licked her, all while gently thrusting his cock into her mouth. A good thing he knew to slide himself back and forth between her lips. Because she was utterly distracted by the attention he lavished on her pussy. He was buried between her thighs, eating her with abandon. And she meant *eat*.

He licked her with humming enjoyment, lapping at her slit, teasing her clit, thrust in some fingers for her to clench as he bit down on her bundle of nerves.

She could only moan and writhe with pleasure while trying to keep from biting him. Still, he suffered a little damage when her orgasm hit suddenly, a rolling wave of pleasure that had her clamping down.

But the climax eased, and she loosened her grip. He kept licking her. Flicking, drawing out the orgasm before he repositioned himself, flipping her onto her belly, then dragging her ass. He slapped his cock off her quivering flesh. She wiggled her ass, and he got the message, sliding into her from behind. Hard. Thick.

Long. Long enough that he hit that sweet spot inside. Once he found it, he couldn't stop tapping it.

Over and over. Hitting her in the place that drew out a short cry and a jolt of pleasure. A slow rhythm at first that turned into a slamming of fleshing. A ramming of his dick that she couldn't get enough of. She moaned for more. Begged. "Harder."

He thrust faster and faster as she clawed at the burlap beneath her. Cried out with passion. Screamed his name when she came.

Came so hard, she collapsed and took a moment to remember how to breathe.

She recovered on his chest, where he'd dragged her. His arms holding her in place. His heart racing as fast as hers.

The realization that he might not be wrong when he'd said that they'd need an eternity to explore whatever was between them had her tensing a bit.

Andrei was her—

Screeeeeeeee.

The metallic scream and the lurch as the train suddenly braked had them stiffening.

"What's happening?" They weren't near any scheduled stops.

"Either there's a problem on the track," Andrei said, "or the train is being hijacked."

Cue the ominous music.

CHAPTER FIFTEEN

The train slowed, a hard brake that made it difficult to put on their clothes as the abruptness of it jolted them. He managed to get his shirt on and slip into his pants before heaving off their bed of burlap. The latest interruption had at least waited long enough for him to touch heaven.

"What will happen once we stop?" Hollie asked, hiding the tattooed flesh he'd stroked. Looking at her, he felt the gouge marks she'd left in his skin. She'd gotten rough when he pleasured her.

Fuck, she was so perfect.

"What happens next depends on the situation. If there is something on the track, they'll have to move it. Could be there's a problem with the rail that requires fixing."

"You also said it might be train pirates."

"It happens. Usually, because they're after a

specific cargo or looking to rob passengers. Don't worry. I won't let them touch you." He had no doubt in his mind now that Hollie was his mate. It brought out the overprotective bear in him.

"Do you think it could be your sister?" she mused aloud.

"It's possible. It would be like her to fuck up plans."

"But can you see her hijacking a train? Sneaking a ride, yes. But taking over the whole thing? She'd never get away with it." Hollie made a valid point.

The train halted as they stood huddled by the door, opened just a crack. *They*, because Hollie refused to hide out of sight. She might not be crazy about the drama, but she didn't back down, either.

Given the train had a few passenger cars, it wasn't surprising to hear shouting. But good news...no screaming. Whatever or whoever had stopped the train wasn't killing anyone.

Yet.

It only took one idiot to start some carnage.

"I'm going to look," she said as she slipped out the door. He reached out too late to halt her.

"Goddamn it, Honeybear," he muttered. How could he protect her if she went ahead? He followed.

The door eased open with only the slightest of whines. He stood on the slim step, dangerous if in motion with its missing railing. Hollie was already standing on the track, peeking around the next car. "I see people," she whispered. "A bunch of them roaming around."

"Any weapons? Vehicles?"

"Nope. I'm going to get closer and see if I can find out what's going on."

"Don't." He spoke to thin air as she slid along the side of the car on the opposite side of where she'd been peeking. Given all the embarkation doors were on the right, she'd doubtless encounter less people.

Meaning, she could move fast. He'd have to move quicker.

Andrei didn't have any disguise to blend in. No time to formulate a plan. He'd have to fake it. He ambled out on the side, milling with people a few cars up from him. Didn't hunch or skulk, simply ambled wide and noticeable to draw any watching eyes to him. Eventually, someone noticed and pointed, a stream of speech following.

He hoped they knew one of the three languages he'd learned. Russian, his mother tongue, English immersion to ensure him fully fluent, and Dothrakian because he liked the guttural sound of it.

He scratched as he neared the gesturing humans. Yawned too for good measure. "Fuck me. Take a nap in an empty car, and you wake up in the middle of fucking nowhere."

"Who are you?" was the heavily accented question. "Where did you come from? It's all cargo at the back."

"It's also quieter than the tiny bench seat I'm

supposed to share with my wife." He grimaced. "I'll take sleeping with the grain over slumbering beside her."

"Sounds like someone needs a new wife." The fellow grinned, and it occurred to Andrei that the man with the accented English was handsome. Best he not lay eyes on Hollie and think he was doing Andrei a favor by trying to steal her.

"Don't touch my woman," he growled.

The man recoiled. "Calm da fuck down. Keep her."

The fellow retreated, and Andrei kept moving until he could see in the train's headlights what had them halted on the tracks. A herd of gazelles, grazing.

Nature at its best.

Smelled delicious.

Maybe he should try bringing one back to their car for a picnic. How would Hollie feel about gazelle tartare?

Even better than gazelle steaks over an open fire? He highly doubted his sister directed a herd to stop the train. Just a coincidence that proved amusing.

People ran at the herd, trying to scatter them, but the skinny-legged beasts were intent on snuffling the ground. A few of the usually meek gazelles even charged the humans. They wouldn't be so brave once they got a whiff of him. He began stalking towards them, determined to help when an unexpected scent caught his nose.

Impossible.

Not here of all places.

It stopped him dead, and he turned, hoping to be wrong. Only to see... "Mama?"

She stood framed in a passenger car, wearing a sensible outfit of dark trousers, a sweater, sturdy shoes, and the expression that said that he had some explaining to do.

"If it isn't my wayward son."

"What a surprise, running into you here." He couldn't help his confusion. How did Mama get on the train before them? No one knew of their plans.

"So, this is where you ran to with your new *friend*." Ah, the subtle insult. So Mama.

"We didn't run. We're here to solve a mystery."

"That involves Nanny Miskouri?" His mother had obviously snuffled out the connection.

"Yes." No point in lying.

His mother's gaze narrowed. "Where is your *friend*?"

Hopefully, staying out of sight. "You shouldn't have come here looking for me."

"Who says I'm here for you? Weren't you the one telling me to do something about your sister?"

His eyes widened. "You're going after Lada?"

"I didn't have a choice." Mama's lips flattened. "Working with humans. Attacking our kind. She's out of control, and she needs to be reined in."

"I'm sorry." He really was. For all his problems

with his sister, he knew his mama took it hard. Probably why she clung so much to Andrei.

"Why would you apologize? It's not as if you failed in raising her." His mother grimaced. "She has too much of her father in her." A different father than Andrei's. Neither of whom had stuck around.

"How did you know to be on this train to find her?" he asked.

"You're not the only one with sources. Apparently, Lada's got two flights booked. One two hours after this train arrives in the city. The other, though, is four hours earlier."

"Why would she have two?" he asked, only to suddenly hear the rumble of motors. Not that of the train.

The people chasing gazelles and milling around having a cigarette began to yell. Screams started as some rushed for the passenger cab, others bolted for the hills.

A pair of all-terrain vehicles came screaming out of nowhere, driving the panic.

But more worrisome was the fact that they appeared to be shooting, and something hit his mother. She yanked the tube poking out of her chest and frowned at it. "What is it?"

"Tranquilizers. Lada must be here." Had to be. She and her gang of henchmen were partial to them as a weapon.

His mother clung to the doorframe, blinking. "I think I need to lie down." He saw her eyeing him expectantly, waiting for him to declare that he'd protect her. He hesitated, though.

Twenty or so feet away, a woman ran screaming, only to drop to the ground as she was hit. Even before she'd fully face-planted, someone jumped out of the side-by-side and rolled her over. Checking her face before moving onto the next limp body. Looking for someone.

Hollie.

Fuck. She was still on the other side of the train.

The choice wasn't easy, but he left his mother in the train car and bolted for the space between it and the next car. He emerged on the other side of the train to spills of light from the windows on board, lots of shadow, and the headlights from the pair of all-terrain vehicles now stopped and idling. By the headlights' beams, he also saw motorbikes close by, the people straddling them armed with guns. But his gaze moved quickly from the weapons to the pair of guys holding a limp body between them.

He didn't need more light to know who they'd kidnapped.

"Honeybear!" he roared as he ran. He felt himself thicken, his claws popping, his jaw expanding to accommodate his more prominent teeth. He didn't go unnoticed.

The attackers shot at him.

Sting. Sting. The darts slammed into him, but he ignored them. He'd had worse when he raided honeycombs.

He kept running, even as those on the ground clambered back onto their ATVs, taking Hollie with them.

He ran for the nearest bike and almost made it, was close enough to recognize his sister's eyes above the bandanna before several more darts hit him.

Too much even for a bear to handle.

CHAPTER SIXTEEN

Disorientation had Hollie lying still as she woke,
resting on her stomach, in a room that smelled
vaguely like her own if she'd let a herd of strangers
trample through it. Impossible. How could she be
home when her last recollection had her on a train in
South America? With Andrei.

They'd... She heated at the thought of what they'd
done. Then she frowned as she recalled the train stop-
ping. Creeping out to a side with only a few people.
Making it a few cars before she heard the sudden rev of
engines. The attackers came roaring out of nowhere,
their sudden beams of light causing confusion as they
raced for the train. Hollie went to hide between the
cars—okay, maybe she had been going to find Andrei—
when they started shooting darts. She might have
gotten away if a frightened human hadn't shoved her
into the open when she went to slide between the cars.

Startled, she'd not ducked in time, and the

attackers had darted her. She'd fallen and blinked heavy lids as she heard feet approaching and someone saying, "Send out the order to round up. Looks like we got lucky and found our target."

She was lifted from the ground and, despite her drugged state, comprehended that they wanted her. For what?

When she struggled, they gave her more drugs, and then everything was a huge blank until now. During that time, she'd been moved and apparently brought home. At least it smelled like her house, the floor the same fake oak laminate she'd installed in her bedroom. However, she knew it wasn't Andrei who'd rescued her. He would have never left her to sleep alone on the floor.

But there *was* the smell of bear nearby. Lada. As to the why...

The damned key. Which really was turning out to be more trouble than it was worth.

Perhaps it was the drugs. Maybe it was her annoyance finally coming to the surface. Whatever the case, her claws came out and dug into the bare floor. The slight movement didn't go unnoticed.

"She's awake," someone announced, shifting from their spot and drawing her attention. A man in jeans and a vest over a dark shirt, stood by the doorway, armed with a tranquilizer gun. So, not trying to kill her. Of course, not. She couldn't help them if she was dead.

But, on the other hand, she had no problem

evening the odds in her favor. After all, before she became a plumber, she used to be a predator.

She sprang to her feet and reached for the suspended light in the ceiling, knowing the guy wouldn't expect it. He shot and missed. He almost managed to aim for a second round when she slammed into him. Her rage allowed her to wrestle away the tranquilizer gun, shoot him with it, and then roll off just as one of his friends entered the room and fired.

He missed.

She didn't.

Two down. And who knew how many were out in the common areas. By now, they knew she was awake and fighting.

She bolted into her living room, out of tranquil-izing darts—not that it mattered. She'd never have been able to fire quickly enough to take out the welcoming committee anyway.

Hollie halted as she saw four guys armed with tranq guns, all aimed at her. But that wasn't the entire reason she froze. Someone who could only be Lada by the scent, sat on her couch. And trussed up beside her like a turkey ready for roasting—

"Mom?"

Green eyes rimmed in gold peered at Hollie. They took stock of the daughter she rarely saw and relaxed. As if Dollie Joliette was worried. The woman lacked a maternal gene and had spent much of Hollie's child-hood avoiding doing the normal stuff other mothers did.

It surprised Hollie to see her. After all, her mother had popped in for a visit just a month ago and then made Hollie ask if Dollie was dying because she called her twice since then, as well.

Dollie looked pissed. So was Hollie, because it was obvious what had to happen next.

She tossed down the empty tranquilizer gun and put her hands up. "You must be Lada."

"And you are clearly the pussycat who's been fucking my brother." The other woman sneered.

"What can I say, all that hair turns me on." And Hollie was a girl with the tools to unclog the drains.

"You know why I'm here. Hand over the key." Lada snapped her fingers.

"What key?" Playing stupid gave her a few more seconds to try and conjure a plan out of thin air.

Lada grabbed Hollie's mother by the hair and yanked. Most people would have yelped, Dollie stared daggers.

It made Hollie wonder... "How the heck did you get captured?"

"She walked right into my hands. Didn't you, pussycat?" Lada smirked.

"I came by for a visit."

"Why?" Because her mother didn't just visit.

"Your aunts mentioned that you'd hooked up with a Medvedev."

"And like a good mother, you suddenly give a damn who I date?" Hollie had issues with her mother, namely the fact that she'd only been around part of the time. Always chasing better things and not bringing Hollie with her. Postcards and gifts from around the world weren't a substitute for a parent.

"I always took care of you."

"Being a parent is more than tossing money at an inconvenience," was Hollie's acerbic reply.

"You shouldn't complain," Lada snapped. "My mother is a controlling maniac."

"According to you. I feel like I should point out that your brother didn't turn out to be a kidnapping psychopath."

"Give it time," Lada spat. "Look at what he's consorting with now."

"You're one to talk. Hanging with humans," Hollie stated, eyeing the men at Lada's back.

"Shut your mouth. Unless you're going to tell us where the key is," Lada snapped.

"House key? Probably wouldn't do you much good since I obviously need new locks."

"Stop fucking with me and give me the goddamned key." Lada's volume exploded, and so did her accent.

"You know, that story in the book is just that," Hollie tried saying, only to bite her lip as Lada back-handed Dollie. Who again, looked more pissed than hurt.

"If it's just a tale, then hand the key over. Why do you care?"

The fact of the matter was, she didn't. "I'll give it to you, but only if you release my mother first."

"You don't call the shots, bitch," a man who'd been

quiet until now, barked. He had military-short hair and a mean expression. "Start talking, or I shoot a limb each time you stall. Starting...now." The asshole then aimed his pistol and shot her mother in the leg.

With a bullet that left a hole that bled. With Dollie's hands tied, she couldn't apply pressure to stop it.

Shock silenced the room for a moment before Lada said quietly, "What are you doing?"

"You're wasting time. I'm fixing it." The sadistic man pointed his gun at her mother's other leg. He would shoot her again; for a key Hollie was really starting to hate. So, why protect it?

"It's under the patio stone in the garden by the composter."

The asshole with the revolver inclined his head, and one of his men went off to look, leaving Lada to hiss, "We said no killing."

"She's not dead. Stop whining, or I'll give you something to whine about."

Lada growled and moved in the asshole's direction, but he redirected his gun. "Do it. You know I'll shoot you."

Before Lada could decide if it was worth her while, the guy returned with the sealed plastic bag containing the key.

"Excellent." The shooter reached for the bag, but Lada snared it first. "Hand it over."

"Don't be so grabby. I'll take the key because you need to watch them for any sudden moves."

"I'll shoot them if they so much as twitch. Maybe I'll shoot them anyway for knowing too much."

"Lord, fucking save me from murderous morons," Lada muttered before turning to the humans. "We need to move before someone notices what happened here."

"I'm not the one running my mouth. Wasting time."

"Let's go."

"In a second. I want to make sure no one follows." As the gun lifted, Hollie's mom swung her foot, and the bullet went wide. But the tranquilizer one of the other guys fired in reflex didn't. Her mom slumped, and Hollie dove back into her bedroom.

Would they come after her?

A door slammed, and she listened for thirty more seconds before realizing that Lada and her band of humans had left.

Hollie flew out to the living room to check on her mother.

"Figures you'd make this the one time in my life you choose to show up," she grumbled as she pressed against her mom's wound. Shifters could heal better than most, but a loss of blood could still kill.

"Better to make an entrance than to not come at all."

Hollie's heart almost stopped as her mother replied. "I would have preferred you show up for my graduation."

"I was doing time in a Mexican prison back then. I sent you flowers."

"Always with the excuses," Hollie declared. She eyed her mother. "How come you're awake?"

Her mother held out her hand and showed the dart within. "I faked it."

"I still can't believe they caught you in the first place."

"You shouldn't be, given how many times I've been arrested. I was never good at the stealthy part."

"Why are you really here?" Hollie asked.

"Because when I got the call that you'd been kidnapped, I panicked."

She blinked at her mom. "You were worried about me?"

"Yeah. What can I say? I'm getting old."

Hollie tried to think of a reply and was saved as the door crashed open, and in rushed her bear.

CHAPTER SEVENTEEN

The door bounced off the wall, as did Andrei's roar. His blood pumped as he scented the intruders and Hollie.

Hollie and a woman who resembled her knelt on the floor, gaping at him.

"Honeybear!" His voice was gruff as he beheld her. Then he went a little ballistic as he smelled the blood. "You're hurt!"

"Not me. My mom." She angled her head to the wound she pressed against.

"My sister shot her?"

Hollie shook her head. "One of her henchmen did. You just missed them."

"Stupid customs delay. I told my mother we should have flown with the cargo," he ranted. He should have moved faster even as it felt as if he'd been rushing since he woke up in his mother's lap on the train. The drugs in the darts he'd been tranqued with took hours to run through his system. Long enough that the passengers had been rounded up and the train was on its way again.

Waking cradled in a lap, a hand stroking his hair, he'd thought for half a second that he'd had a bad nightmare until he opened his eyes and saw his mother.

His subsequent yodel didn't impress, and Mama had dumped him off her lap. Still groggy at the time, he'd rolled to his feet and noticed that they were in a hotel room. Shabby but large. Missing one crucial detail.

"Where's Hollie?" he'd asked his mother.

"That's what you want to ask? Not, 'how are you, Mama?' Are you okay?'" She'd grabbed her chest over her heart.

"Lada took my honeybear." he'd grimly announced, but he knew where she'd be going because there was only one reason to take Hollie.

The fucking key.

Now, seeing his lion on her knees on the floor, covered in blood, his heart stopped.

"Honeybear!" he threw himself at her. Only to have her squeak, "Careful."

He slowed down his approach but still put his hands on her to check her out. "Again, I'm fine. I wasn't the one shot," she assured.

He eyed the woman on the floor, who had an intense stare. "Hello, Hollie's mama."

"Don't you hello me, bear. I will be your worst nightmare if you hurt my daughter," the woman stated.

"Mom!" Hollie exclaimed. "Would you not start. You're like twenty years too late. Speaking of late, your timing could have been better," she snarked at Andrei.

"Did my sister get the key?"

Hollie bit her lower lip and nodded. "I had no choice. They shot my mom."

"I'm sorry. This is my fault."

"How? You only tried to help."

"I should have been faster. But my mother insisted that we fly first class, and when I tried to sneak into the baggage area, she had the airport dogs sniff me out," he grumbled.

"This is the bear you've been hanging with?" Hollie's mother asked. She pursed her lips. "Don't tell me you're a mama's boy."

"At least his mother loves him," snapped Hollie. "I need a knife."

He didn't ask what for. If she felt the need to kill her mother, he'd help her hide the evidence. Instead, she sliced her mother's wrist restraints, then ripped her pants open to check on her wound. "It's a clean in and out. Keep applying pressure until it stops," she said before standing.

"Where are you going?"

"Andrei and I have some villains to interrogate."

"We do?" he asked. "I thought I just missed them."

"You did, but I've got a pair of them drooling in my bedroom that might be able to answer some questions."

"What?" He might have roared again, but only a little.

"Come on, Papa Bear, and save that scowl for the questioning."

The problem? The men were out cold, and no amount of slapping or cold water would wake them.

Right about when he was about to give up, Hollie's mom snarled, "Take one more step, and I'll shoot!"

Hollie's eyes widened.

Then his followed suit as he heard the reply. "Better not miss, or I will eat your face."

Andrei's gaze met Hollie's in shock as their mothers met in person.

"Oh, shit." They scrambled for the living room to find their mothers facing off.

"So, you're the sow who birthed the meathead my daughter's been hooking up with," Dollie said with a hint of salt.

His mother retaliated with, "At least my son doesn't have to come to my rescue because I'm incompetent."

"Incompetent says the prima donna who arrived too late. I, at least, had the common sense to tag the attackers so we could track them. What did you do?"

"Um, Mom, what did you say?" Hollie interjected.

"I might have gotten taken by surprise, but I am not completely useless. I slid my key tracker into a human's pocket when they weren't paying attention."

It was Andrei who yelled, "What the fuck are we waiting for?"

"I need a phone to log in with. Duh," was the reply.

Andrei's mother was the one to hand over a phone

and he tried not to pace impatiently as Hollie's mom tried to type one-handed because the other was still holding her wound.

"Give me that." His mama snatched the cell and barked, "Give me the login info."

Once they had the app loaded, Hollie grabbed the phone. "Gotta go."

"Wait, what about me?" asked Hollie's mom.

"Mama will take care of you, won't you?" Andrei said. "After all, she used to be a nurse."

"Midwife."

"It involves blood," was his reply as he snared Hollie's hand.

"Don't you touch me," Hollie's mom exclaimed.

"Is your daughter as cowardly as you?" The expected sneer came with the retort.

"My daughter is much too good for your son."

While their mothers proceeded to explain why their kid was better, Andrei and Hollie headed out the door, but she avoided the car and set off on foot.

"What are you doing?"

"They appear to have stopped." She pointed to a spot a few blocks away. They ran, hand in hand, his blood pressure finally easing, his bear calming now that he was reunited with his mate.

And to hell with his mother if she didn't like it. He'd told her while she was mid-rant, and over the ocean at a zillion feet where he couldn't jump out, that he would be marrying *that cat*. Then used the only threat he could think of that might halt Mama in her tracks.

"Either accept Hollie, or you won't meet your grandchildren."

Mama's mouth snapped shut. "You really are serious about that girl?"

"She's my mate. My life is bound with hers, which means either you accept her, or..."

Mama held up her hand. "Don't say it. I can't hear it." His mother shut her eyes. Heaved a deep breath, and on a long-suffering sigh, said, "If I must, then I will welcome your chosen bride with open arms. I shall teach her how to cook and please your never-ending appetite. I will tell her all my tricks for keeping a husband happy, even the one with the cherry and that tongue trick that drives men—"

"Ack!" He'd put his hands over his ears at that point. Although, he doubted things would be smooth sailing given their mothers appeared ready-made to hate each other. It would make family gatherings interesting.

Their feet pounded the pavement as they reached the SUV with its dark-tinted windows, parked on the side of the road. A man lay bleeding inside, holding his gashed leg as he gaped at them.

"What happened?" Andrei snapped.

The human blubbered. "Her eyes started glowing, and she scratched me." He glanced down at the gouges. "With giant claws."

"Where did they go?"

"I...I don't know."

But Andrei did. And so did Hollie. They followed the scent of his sister and three other humans. In the distance, he saw them, standing on the bridge. Lada had her back to the railing, facing off against three men. All armed.

"I think your sister is mutinying," Hollie muttered.

Lada held up the key and dangled it over the railing, probably the only reason they hadn't shot her yet.

Andrei and Hollie put on a burst of speed, but he already knew he wouldn't make it in time. He shouted his sister's name. "Lada."

His sister startled and glanced in his direction. It was only a second but enough to set things in motion.

A shot was fired.

His sister yelped.

The key dropped over the bridge railing to the stunned shock of those watching, especially his sister, who screamed, "No!"

And then he was the one to whisper, "No," as red blossomed on his sister's chest. One of the humans had shot her.

As if Lada would die quietly. She turned on her treacherous allies. With a scream of rage, she dove at the guy who'd shot her. And they both went off the other side of the bridge.

What did Andrei do? It was his sister. He jumped in after her.

He searched the flowing river until the sirens sounded in the distance, local law enforcement having been called about shots fired. Only there was nothing to see because the SUV was already gone. His mother had wiped up the blood, and as for the bodies in Hollie's bedroom? The Pride took them in for questioning.

Not that it mattered anymore. He'd failed to save his sister and felt numb inside.

His soaking ass sat shivering on Hollie's couch. His mother, sobbing and ranting, tried to cook, but there was nothing to bake with. No blankets or towels to be found, given the break-in before their trip. Hollie's mom—"Call me Dollie"—had stopped the bleeding using a curtain panel.

They were a ragtag bunch for sure. Then, Hollie declared, "We can't stay here." She took charge, dumping both their mothers on her Aunt Lena's doorstep. Still arguing. A good sign. His mother usually killed the people she really hated. And while she was probably sad about Lada, the truth was, they'd lost her a long time ago.

"Where are we going?" he asked as Hollie drove off with a sigh of relief.

"I pulled some strings and got us booked into a penthouse suite at the Pride Group's hotel."

"I'll bet that wasn't cheap."

"It wasn't, hence why I told them to charge it to you." She flashed him an impish smile.

"I don't suppose that suite has a soaker tub?" he asked with too much hope.

She shuddered. "You know cats hate baths."

"Does that mean you won't join me?"

She turned a serious gaze on him. "Are you sure you're ready for that?"

"If you mean am I a grieving mess over my sister? No. Sad, yes, but I'll get over it. And more because I know how this will hurt my mother. Lada and I were never close. Especially in the last decade."

"So that was your famous mother. She doesn't seem too bad."

He snorted. "Wait until you get to know her. Speaking of which, why did I get the impression yours was dead?"

"More like absent. Which is why her showing up tonight was a surprise."

"Are you sure you don't want to be with her?"

"Very sure. There's only one person I want to be with. Even if he's chaos personified."

"I promise my life isn't always this adventurous."

"And mine isn't always dull. Those alligators in the sewers can get pretty big."

His expression brightened. "Wait until you see the things living in the tunnels under St. Petersburg."

"Am I going to see St. Petersburg?"

"Does a bear wipe his ass with only three-ply?"

"You know that stuff's horrible on pipes, right?"

He laughed and reached for her hand. Squeezed it. And this was why he'd fallen in love.

Given the hotel had sent her an electronic keycard, they could go straight upstairs. The first thing he did after locking the door and shoving a chair under the knob for good measure was to draw a bath.

Despite her assertion about cats hating them, he didn't need to argue to get her to immerse herself in it, her face relaxing as she sighed in pleasure.

Dunking her head, she squirmed under the surface before she emerged with a flip of her hair, spraying him with water. He uttered a teasing growl. "You got my shirt wet."

She tapped the tub. "Then maybe you should take it off and join me."

"Will you wash my back?"

"Will you wash mine?" She turned and peeked at him coyly over her shoulder.

He joined her, the water rising precariously high and sloshing slightly over the sides.

Grabbing a rag and some soap, she scooted in the large tub until she straddled him, then rubbed his upper chest.

He chose to return the favor by dumping soap into her hair, massaging the strands and her scalp, doing it so well that her head tipped back, and she purred as he stroked her. Those soapy fingers drifted from her crown to her shoulders, then teased down her hands, leaving a trail of suds on her skin.

The handheld faucet suddenly turned on, the sudden jet of water drawing a gasp from her, then a sigh as he rinsed her clean. He stood her from the dirty water and kept sluicing her until all the traces of the soap were gone.

Only then did he finally indulge, his mouth clamping onto an erect bud, tugging and sucking at the tip, making her arch and gasp and thrust against him.

She threaded her fingers into the wet strands of his hair, tugged it, an enjoyable pain that caused him to hum as he suctioned, his hands grasping and massaging her flesh.

The brush of her fingers over his cock, so thick and hard, had him eager for what came next. Especially when he teased the swollen flesh between her thighs.

The water got in his way, so he sat her on the wide, marble edge of the tub, spreading her thighs to expose her. His fingers slid into her pussy, thrusting, pushing, filling her, teasing, and getting his enjoyment from her reaction.

He couldn't stop staring at her. At how she gazed back at him with eyes half-shuttered with passion.

His thumb brushed at her sensitive clit, pinched and rolled it, drawing a cry from her lips. Her hips bucked, and then her orgasm hit, fast and hard, pulling forth a scream as her body bowed with pleasure. He kept her from falling as she gasped with pleasure, pulsing around his fingers.

And then it was his turn to throw back his head and suck in a breath as she slid back into the tub, and her fingers curled around him.

He glanced down and watched the slide of her hand back and forth on his dick. The tip of her tongue flicked out, licking her lower lip and drawing a groan from him.

His hips thrust in time to her caressing motion, and he pulsed when she gave him an extra squeeze at the tip.

But he wanted more than for her to jerk him to orgasm. He needed to fill her with his cock. Make her scream as she came again.

Apparently, they were of one mind, because she stood, a streaming wet goddess. "Let's find a bed for once."

He wasn't about to argue, especially given she tugged him to the bedroom, dragging him by his length. He sat on the edge of the bed at her urging, and she leaned between his legs, still stroking. But he was done being a passive participant. He reached out to caress her breasts, the nubs hardening instantly, begging for his attention.

He didn't resist. He leaned in and took the tip of her breast between his lips, biting down lightly, drawing a soft cry from her lips. Grabbing her suddenly around the waist, he tossed her onto the bed and covered her with his body. His mouth found hers as her legs spread in invitation. His cock slid in with a single smooth stroke. A deep thrust, the kind that hit that her sensitive spot.

In and out he thrust, until she panted in pleasure. She clutched at him, digging her nails into his shoulders and back, urging him on, her legs spread wide that he might drive even deeper.

And harder. Over and over, until she shattered.

Came hard on his cock, her lips buried against his shoulder, biting him, marking him as hers.

He did the same, curving his body so that he might latch on to the soft flesh at the top of her breast. Biting her as he came. Joining them body, blood, and soul.

After a second shower that actually cleaned, they ordered room service. And had sex again. In the bed. The shower. On the floor.

She was sleeping on his chest when something woke him. A whisper of sound that had him alert. She stiffened. "Did you hear that?" she whispered against his ear.

Yeah. He'd heard it. Arguing from outside the suite's bedroom door.

"What are you doing here?" hissed Hollie's mother.

"I would ask the same of you, Mrs. Oh I'm Just Popping Out To The Store To Get More Bandages."

"You said you were going to have breakfast."

"I am. With my son."

"Pretty sure they don't want to be disturbed."

"Then why are you here?" grumbled his mama.

"I'm here to make sure you don't interfere with my baby girl's love life."

"Well, I am looking after my son."

"Cut the apron strings. He's her mate. And the future daddy of my grandbabies."

"Don't you mean *our* grandbabies? Or should I say mostly mine, since rumor has it you're rarely around," was his mama's pointed reply.

"I've decided it's time I slowed down and made up for lost time. After all, someone needs to be the fun granny."

"I'm fun."

"You're both loud and annoying!" was what Andrei bellowed.

Whereas Hollie giggled until her mother said, "Now you've done it. You've woken them. So much for them working on making us grandkids."

He could feel the heat in Hollie's cheeks without even seeing it. Especially since they would have most definitely been fucking if not for the interruption.

"If I remember correctly, there's a daily flight leaving in an hour for Italy," he whispered.

"What are we waiting for?" Hollie replied. "Doesn't Italy have some of the oldest plumbing in the world?"

And gondola rides that tipped when rocked too hard. Swimming to shore wasn't the problem. Getting out naked was what got them chased by the cops.

EPILOGUE

Lada's body and the key were never recovered, which Hollie heard an earful about from the aunts. *How could you lose it? You had one job!*

The book disappeared too, meaning they were stuck when it came to solving the mystery of the relic. On a positive note, the attacks ceased, and Hollie agreed with Andrei when he said that whatever secret it led to was probably best left buried.

Life might have returned to boring if she'd actually managed to tame the bear she'd chosen to love, but Andrei wasn't one to do things the normal way. Since she wanted to work, he decided it was time to get into the landlord business. He bought a few rundown buildings that required massive retrofitting and hired her to do all the plumbing.

"Are you nuts? Have you seen the size of the job?" she exclaimed.

"Does this mean you don't want to hear about the

one I bought in Russia?" Because he planned for them to split their time between the two countries.

And she was okay with that. Despite a rocky start, she got along very well with his mama. She'd never had the kind of mother who took her shopping or to the hairdressers or wanted to watch romantic comedies.

The first time she'd taken Mama's side against Andrei, she thought he'd had a heart attack. He'd said nothing for a few minutes before grumbling. And, yes, it was weird having his mother along for their romantic Valentine's Day dinner. Still, she made up for it later with the most epic blowjob he'd ever experienced. Being a plumber, she knew all about suction and pipes —but that didn't mean she'd ever agree for them to dress up as Mario and Peach. She had no interest in having a mustache.

As for her mother...she'd kept her threat about getting closer to Hollie, and when her daughter didn't cooperate, conspired with her mate.

When all was said and done, life was just about perfect. Especially after she had a talk with her bear about leaving the beehives in the woods instead of bringing them home.

He got on board with the packaged variety of honey after she bought a jar and dribbled the amber sweetness all over her body with the demand that he lick her clean.

And for those who wondered, he had the most excellent, prehensile tongue.

TIME TO MOVE ON.

The heavy metal key went into an inner pocket with a zipper so it wouldn't accidentally fall out, along with a flint, and some chalk. In the larger section went his clothes, extra footwear, and protein bars. Peter would have taken the old book of fairy tales with him; however, at its age and size, the pictures he'd stored in a cloud online would be more practical.

He'd spent a lot of time tracking down one of the surviving tomes with the story and illustrations. Only five reproductions had been made—with three of them thought to be destroyed.

Possibly four, given the rumor he'd recently heard. And with the loss of the fake key, interest in it had waned.

Yes, fake.

People had been chasing after the imitation key he'd planted in his Russian apartment before his incident. No one had ever suspected that the real one had been waiting for him in a postal box back home.

With all his things packed, including his passport with his new alias, Peter swung the knapsack onto his back and then climbed out of his window onto the fire escape. Time for a stealthy exit since he didn't want his constant shadow tailing him.

Not where he was going.

He was pretty sure his sister's new husband was

the one who'd hired the duo currently keeping a watch over him. The dour-looking fellow who did the early morning shift to dinner, and the hot gal who had the nighttime surveillance. To protect or to confine? Didn't matter. He wouldn't allow them to get in his way.

Peter thought he'd made a clean getaway until the morning after his arrival in Switzerland, when he woke to a weight on his chest and a purring voice that said, "Where do you think you're going, Peter?"

Nora knows Peter is up to no good, which is why she is following him. But he's wily and sexy for a human she'll discover as they embark on a **Lion's Quest.**

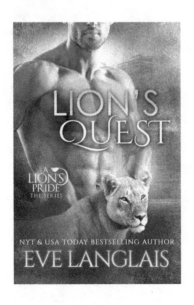

More books in A Lion's Pride:

CPSIA information can be obtained
at www.ICGtesting.com
Printed in the USA
BVHW070115140421
604815BV00008B/447